The House of Remember When

The House of Remember When.
Copyright © 2020 by Scott Jameson Sanders.

All rights reserved. No part of this book may be reproduced in any form or by any electronic or mechanical means, including information storage and retrieval systems, without permission in writing from the publisher and author, except by reviewers, who may quote brief passages in a review.

This publication contains the opinions and ideas of its author. It is intended to provide helpful and informative material on the subjects addressed in the publication. The author and publisher specifically disclaim all responsibility for any liability, loss, or risk, personal or otherwise, which is incurred as a consequence, directly or indirectly, of the use and application of any of the contents of this book.

ISBN-13:
978-1-952405-82-2   [Paperback Edition]
978-1-952405-81-5   [eBook Edition]

Printed and bound in The United States of America.

Published by
The Mulberry Books, LLC.
8330 E Quincy Avenue,
Denver CO 80237
themulberrybooks.com

The House *of* Remember When

A NOVEL BY SCOTT JAMESON SANDERS

Preface

It was the fifth inning and the other team's best hitter was at the plate. He was a left-handed batter and I played right field, so I knew to be prepared for the ball to come my way. There was one out. I was fifteen years old that year and only a sophomore, but I started for the high school varsity baseball team. We weren't that good, but I was having a decent year for a kid who didn't work at the skills of the game very much. Nevertheless, the coach believed in me and let me start in the outfield even though I wasn't a very good fielder. I learned later in life that I had a vision issue in my right eye that affected my ability to judge distance. This is not a good thing for an outfielder. But in those days, right field was the area where the least amount of hits traveled (given that most hitters were right-handed, and they usually pulled the ball to the left side). As a result, I often went full games with nothing more to do than chew on a blade of grass and daydream.

But this guy at the plate was big and he was left-handed, and we knew from the scouting report that he had good power. There was a runner at first who had walked in the previous at bat. My coach motioned for me to move back a few steps, so I backed up extra deep as it would be easier to come in on the ball than to go back. For the first two pitches, our pitcher was trying to keep the ball away so the batter couldn't make too much contact if he hit it at all. And walking him would not be the worst thing. There was already one out with only one on, so no need to give him anything good to hit. But the third pitch of the at bat was a mistake. It was a fast ball that leaked out over the middle of the plate and the batter swung and connected solidly with the ball. I knew instantly that it was coming my way and that it had been hit well. I started running back as the towering shot traveled toward me. But this was more than hit well. This ball had been crushed.

It was a home game for us and strangely, the varsity field at our school had no outfield fence. The only barrier in right field was a street, but it was very far back and down a small declining hill. So home runs on this field were mostly a matter of the speed of the runner as all hit balls (normally no matter how far they went) could be retrieved and thrown back into the field of play. Thus, there really wasn't much of a limit on how far back I could run unless I hit the street . . . which was so far out it had never been reached by a hit ball in a game.

The ball continued to travel toward me and I ran back farther and farther. At this point, I wasn't sure if I could get to it, but I continued running back and then suddenly I felt that the flat surface of the outfield become harder. And then I felt my steps start to descend and I realized that I had somehow reached the hill that angled down toward the street. The ball was very close to me now, but I wasn't sure what to do. If I kept running, I could run into the street and slip or even be hit by a car. Instinctively, I threw my left arm up toward the ball that was now arcing its way down to me. And then the seemingly impossible happened. The ball hit solidly into my glove and I closed my grip around it before hitting the street pavement ahead.

I turned around and saw my coach yelling something and waving his arms to have me throw the ball back. It was either too far away to hear him or I was still in a daze from catching the ball. I ran up the hill and threw the ball as far as I could. It was a terrible throw that curved badly away from the cut-off man and toward second base. But it was then that I realized that the guy who started on first had already rounded second and was heading to third. He could not have imagined that I would catch that ball. It would have been a home run easily at any other field with a fence. To this day, I don't think anyone thought I could catch it, much less catch up to it. Yet, despite my poor

The House of Remember When

nd the feeling I had for several days and weeks after. If it could have een on video, I know I would replay it often, but video cameras were ot yet common in those days. It is one of my favorite memories and can replay it in my mind as often as I want. No one can take that ccomplishment away from me. If only there were a way to bottle that eeling so you could keep it with you, especially when times get tough. nd we all know that no matter who you are, life is going to totally ick you in the ass at some point. This story is about one of those times.

throw, there was still plenty of time for the second basem[an]
the ball and double off the man who started at first base.
Three outs.

As I jogged back to the dugout, I first noticed the [look of]
my coach. Then the other players came up and patted me

"Great catch," remarked the coach. "Nicely done."

"Great play man," shouted an elder teammate as he [slapped]
the back. "How the hell did you catch that thing?!? Fuck[...]

"All right, guys, let's use this as motivation to get b[ack in the]
game. Come on now. Let's get some runs!" the coach sho[uted,]
beaming with joy.

I took a seat on the bench before I was nudged by ou[r coach;]
it was my turn to bat. I was still in a fog wondering if i[t really]
happened. I was not the guy who made the great play [or the]
last second shot to win a game. I was an average ath[lete with less]
than average confidence. But this had truly happened, [and I knew]
then that it was a big deal. People would be talking abou[t it at]
school the next day and maybe for a while after that. I la[advanced?]
to the plate with my bat and considered this could be a [moment I]
might never forget. And I never have.

"Excuse me, son," the umpire said in a friendly mann[er, "you have]
[t]o wear a helmet to get into the batter's box."

I felt the top of my head and turned to see man[y of the play]
[e]rs on my team laughing that I had forgotten to we[ar my hel]
[me]t. That woke me up a bit out of my euphoric da[ze for]
[su]re. At least I didn't forget to bring the bat. I di[d forget]
[things] a lot in those days, but it didn't change the [fact I caught a]
ball that no one thought could be caught.

[I don't re]member if we won the game or if I di[d anything else]
[in that game] or even that season. But I will never fo[rget...]

Chapter 1

TIME IS LINEAR, LIFE IS NOT

What would you do if you learned that there was a way to go back in time? If you could, would you choose to go back and relive one of the best moments of your life? Or would you choose instead to correct some past wrongs? Would you want to meet an important religious or historical figure? Jesus? Mohammed? Mr. Rogers? Would you go back to a significant event in your life? We all think about it, right?

Many books and films from the past have explored this time travel topic with incredible creativity. I love these stories, but no matter how they describe the time-traveling experience, there is a critical flaw in all of them. Put simply, it is impossible and against the law of nature as we know it to go back in time. Once we have lived the moment, the moment is past and gone forever and it becomes history. And besides, even if we could go back, it is also impossible to relive a moment without having it change the previous outcome. Or worse, it would change the future in some dramatic way and everything you know could be negatively affected. So, time travel is a myth and all these tales we like so much are just enjoyable fiction because time travel is impossible. That is what I believed, that is, until the day I entered the strange looking house with the green door at the end of my street.

In early November, in the eastern suburbs of Cleveland, the sun rises at approximately seven o'clock in the morning. Unfortunately for me, my dog has to relieve herself one hour preceding that, so I am left to walk her in the virtual darkness of the late fall mornings. On some lucky days, however, the light of the moon can sneak through the ever-present clouds in northeastern Ohio. And that was the case this fall morning as I walked Dingo down the full length of our suburban street.

As I strolled sleepily along Sterncrest Avenue, Dingo did her normal smelling of every weed, rock, and twig in our path. Our dog was a classic mutt and, yes, I named her that because of the Meryl Streep movie. I thought it was funny and no one in the family argued with me about it, so the name stuck. She was a good dog and, in many ways, my best friend. She loved me unconditionally and I still marvel at how dogs never seem to be in a bad mood. I have had a dog my entire life and still dream about my childhood dog, Gordon, who died when I went off to college. I was heartbroken when I found out he had passed away. He was a rescued mutt too and had a nasty habit of biting people for no good reason, including me, but I loved him anyway. I'm still not completely over that loss, but I vowed back then to always adopt a rescued mutt, and Dingo was no exception.

My goal on our early morning walks was to get Dingo to do her business as quickly as possible so I could return to get my essential hot cup of morning tea. But Dingo is smart. She knows not to urinate too quickly, or I would immediately turn around and head back home. My eyes were only half-open this morning as I gazed ahead at the rows of mostly colonial homes that lined both sides of our street. Our neighborhood is a typical Midwestern middle-class suburb, except that our street contains homes on unusually large lots. For the most part, the smallish houses just don't seem to fit the expansive lawns in front of them. This characteristic also leads to a neighborhood where people don't congregate together very much. The ample spacing between homes provides plenty of neighborly insulation, and truthfully, I like it that way.

On most of my walks, I like to keep to a familiar pattern and I usually turn right at the end of Sterncrest onto Jackson Lane. But today, Dingo wanted to turn left for some reason. She jerked at the leash relentlessly until I agreed and shifted my course westward. In this direction, there is a house at the end of the street that has a dimly lit green front door. It is an interesting shade of green that really stands out. The hue reminds me of many cars from the '70s which fits with the house's outdated style of architecture. The structure itself is a white-plank ranch-style home with two dormers and a small chimney on the east side. It is smaller than most of the other nearby homes and with no particular charm except that it marks the end of Jackson Lane. Thus, as you walk down this street, you walk directly toward the green door of this old home. In my twelve years of living here, I had never seen anyone enter or leave this house. I heard once that an old woman had left it for her children, but none of them had come to claim it. I had occasionally seen someone outside to cut the grass, but the once-manicured gardens and hedges were now all overgrown.

As Dingo (the dog) and I approached the end of the street, I gazed ahead at the house wondering why no one had ever thought to move in or renovate it. Our neighborhood is a desirable place to live, with better-than-average schools and a reputation for being relatively safe. Plus, a house that is ignored for too long starts to look strangely sad as if it knows it has not been loved or cared for. It fascinated me to think that no one lived there and yet the property wasn't even for sale. In my opinion, the house looked . . . lonesome. Was there an out-of-town relative who simply paid to keep the grass cut? If so, why wouldn't he want to sell it? Was there some sentimental attachment to the house? Or could it be that the house was cursed and that whoever had lived in it went totally insane. As I continued to ponder the myriad possibilities, my thoughts were interrupted by Dingo barking at the front door of the old home.

"Shhh. Dingo!" I said to my dog, thinking that I might at least pretend to appear concerned that someone in the neighborhood could still be sleeping.

I looked around and up and down the empty street as the orange sun began to peek through the clouds. Dingo was pulling me toward the house for some reason and this was something she had never done before. Giving in to her, I started up the front walk toward the door of the solemn and potentially cursed old house. *What the heck am I doing?* I thought to myself. There could be people watching me. This could even be against the law and who knows what lurks inside there?

I don't believe in ghosts, goblins or spirits, but I have no desire to test the supposition either. Was I nervous? Sure. In my opinion, it is smart to have a healthy fear of certain things. For example, I have an enormous fear of bungee jumping. I mean, who in their right mind volunteers to be the first to try out the bungee cord? What if the rubber line is slightly too long for the drop? Don't rubber bands stretch and break over time? If you keep using it, won't it be ready to snap someday? Again, no matter how safe they say it is, I am not going to bungee jump. And usually I felt the same about entering a potentially haunted house. Nevertheless, I continued to let Dingo pull me along toward the front door.

When I got to the front stoop, I looked at the flickering yellow light above the door. The paint on the ceiling above was peeling and there was a small window in the top panel of the door. Beneath it was a tarnished brass knocker. I stepped up and peered into the small window opening on the door. The inside entryway was devoid of pictures and furniture and all I could clearly make out was a dark wooden staircase. There was one couch and a ladder-back chair in the front room, but no other ornamentation. There were several closed doors down the main corridor and I noticed that one of them had a broken door handle. The old rusted door knob lay in solitude on the floor below looking like one of those antique artifacts from the sunken Titanic.

"Very strange," I said out loud as Dingo scratched at the doorframe. I tried to tug her back to continue our walk, but she continued to hold firm and pull towards the door. She wanted in there, but why? Why today? We had been down this street before and she had never wanted to go in. What was inside? We all know that dogs have these incredible instincts that defy human logic. Like when dogs sense danger and do amazingly heroic acts to save their masters. And then there was that lost dog that walked across the entire country to find his relocated family. Dogs are simply amazing. So maybe there was something in there that I needed to see. If true, shouldn't we go in? Or what if there was something wrong with someone inside and I needed to find out what it was? I have a responsibility to do that, right? But there is also a penalty for trespassing, and I was already on the verge of voyeurism and I'm pretty sure that is illegal.

"Forget it, girl. Not today," I said to Dingo as I tugged on her leash to turn around and head back down the street. As we walked along, I sensed a strange feeling inside, like I had eaten an old hot dog or some bad chili. I knew that feeling had to do with that house and it left me wondering why suddenly out of nowhere, I just had to go look inside. Dingo seemed to feel the same way as she continued to look back as if she had left a bone back there on the stoop. What was it that drew us and made us both so curious? I was scared and uncertain, but I knew I would go back. I had to go back. And when I did, I discovered far more than I could have ever imagined.

Chapter 2

LIFE IS LIKE A CROSSWORD PUZZLE (WE FIGURE OUT THE PIECES AS WE GO)

My wife and kids were all at the kitchen table when I returned. I had been gone a full hour, which is significantly longer than my normal morning dog walk. My wife, Rachel, was doing the usual weekday routine, which included yelling at the kids to stop fiddling and finish their breakfast. My two girls were arguing about something when I arrived. I entered the room with Dingo, who proceeded to make a dash for her water dish. I had obviously missed breakfast as the plates on the table were mostly empty.

"What took you so long?" my wife asked indignantly.

"Nothin'," I said back to Rachel, who was now putting dishes into the dishwasher.

"I thought you got mugged or something."

"No. Not mugged, but there was a house on fire down the street. Fortunately, I was able to save everyone inside and put it out with a neighbor's garden hose. Dingo helped too. She saved their cats, but then chased them down the street. I hope they find them. Right, Dingo?" I uttered as she lapped and slopped water all over the kitchen floor.

Rachel continued to clear the table as if I had said nothing. My wife is a highly motivated "type A" individual, and my theory is that she [   ] literally does not have the time for my sense of humor. Either [   ] am not very funny.

"Do you know if anyone has ever lived in that house at the end of Jackson?" I inquired as I moved toward the cupboard to get a mug for my tea.

"What house?"

"The one with the green-colored door. The one—oh, you know, that looks haunted."

"How should I know?" Rachel stated mindlessly while I dipped a tea bag into a cup of hot water.

"I just looked into the window and it's empty. Nothing in there but an old wooden chair and dirty couch. I've never seen anyone go in or out. Have you?"

"Is that what took you so long? Peering into empty houses?" Rachel remarked with disgust. "Honestly, I have never paid it any attention, but someone should clear the lawn of debris occasionally. It's a mess. I hate it when one bad apple spoils the whole neighborhood."

In addition to being a type A, my wife is also a freak about proper appearances. To me, I couldn't care less if someone a quarter mile away wanted to paint their house hot pink or put gnomes all over the yard.

"What bad apple? What do you mean?" my nine-year-old daughter, Mary, asked as I sat at the table and jerked a green permanent marker out of her hand.

"Dad! I need that!" Mary barked as she attempted to grab it back from me.

"No, sweetie. The ink goes right through the paper and onto the table. See?"

I pointed at an ink stain in the area where she was writing. Our once-proud kitchen table has seen its better days. I wasn't totally sure if I was pointing at the right mark, but I pretended to be confident that this mark was the correct one for today.

"I had the marker first and she took it from me," Jessica interjected. "Mommy says that I can use them, but only if I put dews-paper down first."

"I'm writing on paper!" Mary exclaimed. "So why would I need a newspaper?"

My daughter, Mary, is the most practical one in the family. She is smart, but like Rachel, she sees no need for humor in life. In addition, she is always correcting us and seems to have the answer for everything. Her maturity defies her youth and tends to drive the rest of us absolutely crazy.

"Just let me have it, Dad. I'm almost finished," Mary stated.

"No, you need to put down dews-paper!" my seven-year-old shouted again through a mouthful of bacon.

Rachel put the dishcloth on her shoulder and turned to sneer at me.

"Are you going to parent here or do I have to do everything?" she stated coldly as she yanked a different marker out of Mary's hand.

"I was going to. I mean, I was trying to . . ."

"Never mind. Girls, please go brush your teeth and put your backpacks in the car. I'll be out there in two minutes. Two minutes and I mean it. Two minutes."

I often think that my wife missed her calling. She would have been an outstanding army drill sergeant. She is thin and pretty, but she can also get the three of us moving with just a look. When I do try to parent my kids, it takes pleading and promising of gifts or fun "surprises" to get those two girls to do anything quickly. But when Rachel turned around to give them the "look," both girls popped out of their seats and started rushing to get ready. As I sat there, I noticed that the clock on the stove was at fifteen minutes past seven. It surprised me too that I had been gone with Dingo for more than an hour. I knew I had felt very strange when I was at that old house. I wondered if I had gone into a time warp or something. I hadn't entered the house with the green door, but I did step onto the front stoop.

The time gap was a mystery to be pondered, but I was quickly bounced out of my deep thinking when a damp dishcloth hit me in the face.

"Did you hear me?" my wife inquired sternly.

"Hear what?" I replied while throwing the dish towel back toward the sink.

"I'm going to the parent-teacher meetings tonight and I need to know if you are going to go with me. If you're planning on playing cards with your tennis buddies, I'll get a babysitter, but you really should go with me to these things. Mary's teacher thinks I'm a single mom. Jessica's conference is next Thursday so put that on your calendar. You've never been to even one of hers. I swear I might as well be alone. You are so detached from everything in this family."

"What the heck did I do?" I asked innocently. "I'm just sitting here and you're already mad at me?"

"That's right. You are always just sitting there. That's exactly the point."

"I'll go to the stupid parent thing. I don't care. Just tell me what you want me to do and I'll do it," I responded defensively.

I never seem to say the right thing when my wife goes into scheduling mode. In seventeen years of marriage, this has been one of our primary sources of conflict. And lately, we seem to have a lot of areas where I am just not measuring up to my wife's expectations. For example, my wife has a phenomenal capacity to keep dates and details in her head and I am exactly the opposite. If I don't write down the event immediately, it is very likely to be forgotten or missed. I also tend to try to interrupt her with questions (mostly asking "Why do we have to do that?"), which only frustrates the process more. So, I am best to just keep quiet, although no matter how hard I try, I think my eyes tend to reflect that I am not listening. I now tell young people who ask me about marriage that "opposites attract, but you better learn to live with being told what to do all the time."

"Just be engaged in the lives of this family. Okay?" my wife said as she picked up the dish towel off the floor.

"Okay," I said just to end the conversation, but I didn't really know what I was agreeing to. My wife often tells me to do more to help her, but when I do, it's never the right thing. For example, if she tells me to get the girls dressed, I will go upstairs and help them pick out their clothes. Mary is very picky about what she wears, but Jessica would wear anything to school and I mean anything. She just picks up the first thing she sees on the floor of her closet and that is the day's attire. Pajama top, rain boots—it really doesn't matter. So, inevitably, Jessie comes down in attire totally inappropriate for school, and Mary will cry out to us that she doesn't have anything to wear. To get Mary moving, you must yell, but I am not a yeller. So I try to help her pick things, but it always takes too long and then Rachel comes up and yells at all of us.

It's not a perfect world, but it would be great if Rachel would ask me to do things that I can successfully accomplish, like changing light bulbs, for example. I can do that, but she always does it before I notice that the lights are out and then complains that she had to do it. She doesn't allow me to paint or decorate any more as my tendency to take shortcuts usually means a half-assed job. I do walk the dog, but she doesn't see that as a contribution as she knows I need exercise and the mental breaks from work or the commotion of the family. So I'm left to wonder what it is that I am supposed to do to help. I know I'm not very handy with fix-it projects and most of my limited energy is spent trying to keep up with my work responsibilities.

After a few sips of my black tea with just a smidge of cream, I heard the back door slam and then the house fell silent except for the sound of Rachel's car starting in the adjacent garage. I looked down at the crossword puzzle and started to read one of the clues when the back door opened, and Rachel reappeared in the kitchen hallway.

"And please, for God's sake, do not forget to take the recycling out. You missed it last week and it is a total mess out here in the garage. I can barely get the car out. And the painters, please don't forget to call them. The front of the house looks like crap. Can you do that one thing for me, please?"

"Sure, but that was more than one thing," I remarked as I grabbed a pencil from the other end of the table.

"Have fun doing your crossword puzzle!" Rachel shouted. "I'll be at the school until noon and then we have Girl Scouts at four."

Rachel disappeared again around the corner and I could literally feel my heartbeat slow precipitously. I released a long sigh as the steam from my tea rose in front of my face.

"Satisfaction," I blurted out.

That was the answer to "What the Stones can't get" on my crossword puzzle.

Chapter 3

LIFE IS NO MORE THAN WHAT YOU PERCEIVE IT TO BE

The phone in my home office rang and woke me up out of a somber sleep. It was 10:15 a.m. and I had been napping on the couch in my office for a good half hour. I got up quickly to look at the caller ID and saw that it was my mother calling from Louisville. I had not talked to her in quite a while, but there usually wasn't much for us to discuss anymore. My father had been retired for ten years and since then my parents' life had become quite mundane. Without any significant hobbies, there was nothing really left for them except their routine of meals, medications, and doctors' appointments. It seemed cruel to me that the reward for a life of hard work and accomplishment was to be so bored that a major surgery would seem like a welcome distraction.

I ignored the call thinking that I was too sleepy to talk and that I would call her back later. I settled into my office chair and stared blankly ahead at the twenty new e-mails that had come in since I last looked at the screen. I'm lucky enough to make a decent living at what I do, but I am not one of those people who loves their job. I used to like it, but that was mostly because it paid well. In the early days, I was motivated to work hard because I love to shop for things my parents would never buy, like nice cars with leather interiors and fancy big televisions. Color televisions. HiDef, big screen, LCD. Yes, it's true. I love to watch television.

When I was a kid, we had one television in the house and it was a small black-and-white set. My father would not even spring for cable when that became available, even though everyone I knew was getting it. He figured that he only needed to watch the network evening news, so why spend money on the frivolous. As a result, I have overcompensated in my home. At last count, we have eight televisions including one in the master bathroom, one for practically every room in the house. And I especially love to watch reruns of my favorite shows. My absolute favorite is the sitcom *Seinfeld*. I lived in New York City after college and I can still relate to almost everything they put those characters through, especially George. He seemed to be patterned after me, having embarrassing things happening to him over and over. I tell people that *Seinfeld* is the *I Love Lucy* of our generation. It never gets old, so I watch it a lot. And a lot means every day.

My job, if you could call it that, is most aptly termed "independent brokering." Some people would call me a professional salesperson, but I no longer work for a single company, so "broker" is the better descriptive title. I like that title more anyway since "sales" can have such a negative connotation. In my experience, many people either hate the idea of being labeled as a "Willy Lowman" sales-guy or they simply fear the idea of cold calling. Either way, they are missing out as it is a relatively easy job once you get the hang of it. You only have to meet people, solve their problems, and pretend like you like them in the process. And I was pretty good at all those things.

And after twenty plus years of doing this for a living, I had built up a lot of repeat customers, so things almost run on their own for me now. I don't have to travel much anymore, and, best of all, I am able to do this job from my home. Unfortunately, the fire to grow my business had been diminishing over the last few years, and I simply don't enjoy the work like I used to in the earlier years. I think it might be because I now have accumulated all the toys and gadgets I want. I could go out and bring in more accounts, but it just doesn't seem worth the effort since there is nothing else that I need. As a result, at this point in my career, I am simply ... bored.

So packaging sales is my chosen vocation, but it didn't start out that way. Prior to graduating from college, I had no idea what I was going to do. I was a history major and almost all my history classmates were planning to go right on to graduate school. I had no desire to do that and found that I only liked portions of history and didn't really enjoy reading that much. And studying history meant a lot of reading. So I went to look for other types of jobs and quickly discovered that I wasn't qualified for anything. So, I pretty much took any job that anyone was willing to offer me. After six years of trying various low-level positions, I finally determined that I needed to go back to school so I could figure out what I was really meant to do. And business school seemed like the logical choice since I surmised that the reading requirements would be minimal.

It turned out that business school was the right choice. It was fun to learn what income statements were and how the stock market worked. I enjoyed economics the most, and it seemed to almost come naturally to me. One significant difference between grad school and undergrad was that this time, I really wanted to learn the stuff. I raised my hand whenever I didn't understand something and made the professor explain it again. I was paying for school myself this go around, and I wanted to get my money's worth. But after two years of study, I still didn't know what I wanted to do for a living. I was a generalist and the business world wanted specialists. It was either accounting, finance, or marketing, and none of those appealed to me enough to pick only one path.

So, the month after finishing up graduate school, I randomly accepted a job with a corrugated box company, and they placed me in their sales training program. My salary was just enough to pay for a one-bedroom apartment and—to my amazement—they provided me a company car. And it was a nice car by my standards of the day, a Ford Fairmont, and even though the car was the most boring moving vehicle ever designed, I loved it. It was new and driving a nice car made me feel like a grown-up as it was even nicer than my father's car. And best of all, it was free.

In the late 1980s, this was the basic job description for those of us in sales: drive around your territory to call on people who buy boxes and get them to buy more boxes. In those days, companies also needed external sales people to handle on-site problems and personal communication since there was no internet or e-mail. And by personal communication, I mean lunch. There were no cell phones back then, so the company trusted that we were actually working when we left the office. Without beepers, blackberries, PDAs, and the like, no one really knew what we did, and we could get away with just about anything. Those "unchecked" days are long gone now as we are never more than a text away from having to respond.

I loved the freedom of the job back then, but I did put in long hours and my sales results soon reflected that effort. I didn't really like the entertainment aspect, but the job evolved as the years progressed and that became less of an issue. Most of what we do today is crisis management and it can almost be done entirely over e-mail. These days, people only pick up the phone as a last resort and when they do call, you must be ready to respond right away. The days of the three-martini lunches are gone, but I never enjoyed them much anyway. I was a problem-solver and my customers liked me for that. They still do, I think.

As I stared down at the e-mails, one of them had a red exclamation point and was entitled NEEDS YOUR ATTENTION IMMEDIATELY. Despite my strong desire to head back to the couch, I opened the e-mail to be informed that I had one "last" opportunity to reduce my pricing on an existing product with one of my customers. It didn't state that my price was too high. This was just a trick used by the computer bidding program to fool suppliers into lowering their price more than they have to in order to keep the business. I hated these automated auctions and wanted to write "Fuck you" in the comment section. *Why not? I'm going to do it,* I thought but was fortunately distracted by the phone ringing again. This time it was a number I didn't recognize, so I picked it up and answered with my standard professional greeting.

"This is Neil Moreland. May I help you?"

"Yes. Hello, Mr. Moreland," the voice said. Since they used the word *mister*, I assumed it was a telemarketer.

"Sorry. I'm not at home right now," I joked and prepared to hang up the phone.

"No sir. Don't hang up. This is Mrs. Jenkins from the school office."

"Oh. Sorry. I thought . . ."

"Is Mrs. Moreland at home?" the voice asked.

"Um, no, why?" I responded.

"I am sorry to report, but your daughter Jessica is ill. She is with the nurse now. Can your wife come to school to pick her up?"

Oh no. Jessie was sick. I immediately popped out of my cozy desk chair.

"I will be right there," I said and hurriedly hung up the phone. As I searched for my wallet, I wondered why she asked for my wife instead of asking me to do it. I had a license. I could drive there. Aren't fathers just as capable of handling a sick child as the mother? Nevertheless, I was emotionally shaken by the thought of one of my girls being sick. My biggest fear in life is the thought of anything bad happening to either one of them. What if they got into an accident? What if that stomachache was actually cancer? I don't even want to think about it as I don't know if I could survive the loss of one of my kids.

While grabbing my jacket, I noticed that I was still wearing a wrinkled red T-shirt that read *The Clapper* on the front of it. I would have to change before entering the school or my daughter would never forgive me. I loved that "Clapper" T-shirt and was always fond of the invention that could turn lights or electronic equipment on or off at the clap of your hands. Why everyone didn't have them throughout the house was beyond me. I felt like the King of Siam walking around my house having appliances obey me with a clap of the hands. Mostly due to my incessant clapping and turning lights off on people as a joke, Rachel had them all removed except for the one in my office. At least, I still got to command that one.

I threw on a wrinkled oxford shirt and some blue jeans. Without the motivation to comb my frizzled hair, I threw a baseball cap on and headed to the school, hoping that little Jessica was okay. It was probably the fact that she ate seven pieces of bacon at breakfast that made her sick. I had watched her shoving in piece after piece while pondering the clue "Sun Recording Artist who married his 13-year-old cousin" on my crossword. I should have stopped her from eating so much, but she is so skinny, and bacon is protein, right? Anyway, I concluded that the bacon was the cause and hoped it was nothing more than that.

"Jerry Lee Lewis," I blurted out as I got into the car to leave. I usually loved it when baffling crossword answers simply came to me without effort. But I was not amused this time as my only thoughts were of Jessica and getting there as soon as I could. When I got to the nurse's office, I saw my daughter sitting up on the table with a smile on her face. It was so great to see her looking happy and . . . not very sick.

"I throwed up, Daddy," she said proudly.

"I heard, sweetie. How do you feel now?" I asked as she hopped down off the table.

"I feeled bad before. Can we get ice cream?"

There is nothing more soothing to a parent than a child asking for something sugary after being sick. If Jessie were to ever refuse a chocolate or sugar treat, we would know for sure that something was very, very wrong with her. Nevertheless, this was a good sign and I smiled as I took her hand to leave. The nurse waved goodbye as we walked out into the hallway. Jessica squeezed my hand tightly as we approached the exit door of the elementary school.

"I threw up in a crash tran," she said as we walked outside. I loved the cuteness of her seven-year-old speech and she knew it. Thus, I never corrected flawed pronunciation even when she became aware of it herself. I used to ask her to say the word *breakfast* as I loved the failed attempts that ranged from "breadsticks" to "frickfast." My older brother would often ask her to say "dump truck," which came out just the way you would think. And he would laugh and point at me as if I was the dumb fuck in the family.

"Hey, Jessie. Did your classmates or teacher see you throw up?" I asked curiously.

"Yep. Brandon threw up once and it went all over the floor." She gleamed. "It was so gross, Dad. And it smelled super icky."

"Throw-up always smells icky, honey," I responded. "If I even smell throw-up, I . . . throw up too."

Jessie giggled at my throwing-up face and then looked up adoringly as we approached the car. "Is Mommy home? Will she let me watch TV?"

"I don't know where Mommy is, honey (even though I actually remembered that she was at the school where she volunteers), but you can watch TV as long as you want. Maybe it would be smart of you to sleep a little and then we can watch cartoons and eat ice cream together."

"Yeah!" Jessica blurted out as I buckled her into the car seat in the back of my Audi (yes, with leather interior). "Can we watch *Junksters?*"

One of our favorite shows is a program where two men go out into the country to find antique stuff that is hidden away in old barns or storage units. The thrill is when they uncover some artifact from the past and they negotiate a deal with the owner to buy it. Mary loves the show too, and we watch it whenever we come across it, but only if Rachel isn't around. Rachel is the television censor in our home and she is strict about letting them watch anything that isn't purposely directed at young children. Clearly, *Junksters* is not aimed at children, but I didn't see any harm in it and I loved the idea of uncovering some valuable relic from the past. Once when I was a kid, I thought it would be a great idea to fill a garbage can full of my toys and bury it for fifty years. I thought of this when I was only ten years old. I'm fifty now and in just ten more years, I could dig it up and sell the stuff for thousands. Man, I wish I had done that.

When we arrived home, Dingo was doing her typical "I gotta pee bad" histrionics in the front hall, so I got the leash and gently placed Jessica down on the couch. I handed her some crackers and a glass of water as that seemed to be the right thing for a stomachache. At least that is what my mother would have given me.

"Sit here, honey, and I'll get you some ice cream when I get back from walking the dog, okay?"

"Okay, Daddy," she said as she snuggled up to a throw pillow.

I smiled lovingly back at her as I attached the leash to Dingo's collar. I enjoyed seeing Jessie smile and a warm feeling came over me as I opened the front door to go outside. As she had earlier, Dingo pulled me relentlessly down the driveway, which reminded me of the experience that morning with the house down the street. When we reached the intersection, both Dingo and I were on the same page as we ventured toward the house with the green door. *Jessie will be okay*, I thought. *I'll just take another quick peek inside.*

In the bright daylight, the house looked very different, and in some ways, very odd. The dormers on the roof were covered with moss and the windows had those cheap pull-down canvas shades that tend to rip and discolor from the sunlight. As we approached the house, I noticed that one of the shades was pulled up slightly. I couldn't be sure, but I didn't remember seeing a shade open before.

This time, the light flowing through the window on the door revealed dark oaken floors and antique brass door fixtures. I looked again at the broken door handle lying on the floor. I hated the instinct that came upon me, but I couldn't resist reaching down to try to open the door. I touched the doorknob with my left hand and instantly recoiled from the coldness of the brass knob. I reached down again and attempted to turn the knob when suddenly a voice seemed to come out of nowhere.

"Please come in, Neil. I've been expecting you," the strange voice said.

I looked to my left and right and didn't see anyone. I looked above and saw only the glare of the sun.

"Please, Neil. Come in. There is no reason to be frightened."

"Who ... who are you?" I implored as I stepped back from the door and looked for a fake rock speaker or something to explain the voice. "Where is the intercom? I don't see one."

"If you enter, I will introduce myself," the voice responded.

"Where are you? Is this a joke?" I asked as I continued to look around me for the source of the voice.

"I'm right inside. Please come in. I'd be much obliged if you would," the voice stated politely.

I cleared my throat as I peered again through the window on the door.

"Are you in there? I don't see you," I said as I looked in and saw nothing but an empty hallway. Strangely, the voice seemed like it was only in my head as the sound had no echo. But I knew it wasn't my imagination either as I would never ever have used the words "much obliged."

"Come on in, Neil. I'm eager to meet you," the voice stated again.

I reached down again for the brass knob, but my nerves would not allow me to turn the knob. I pulled my hand away from the door.

"I'm sorry. I can't. I, uh ... I have to walk the dog and ... you see, it's my daughter. She's at home sick."

"Jessica will be fine. And your dog will be fine too. Dingo can come in. I love dogs," the voice said as I blinked my eyes to try to clear my mind.

"Hey, how did you . . . who? "I could feel my heart beating profoundly within my chest. How did the voice know their names?

"I tell you what, I will come back later. Maybe tomorrow. Is that okay? I mean. I want to be sure Jessie is all right. And . . . how did you know her name was Jessica anyway?" I inquired as I tried to exude some confidence in a situation that I clearly did not understand. "Besides, I'm not sure what is going on in there. How do I know you aren't some psycho nut job who wants to chop me into hamburger meat? I can't see you and this is freaking me out a little."

"I assure you. I am not a psycho nut job and I'm not going to hurt you," the voice stated with conviction.

"How am I supposed to know that?" I asked.

There was no response to my question, so I nervously backed farther away from the door. I looked around again and then down at Dingo who was looking up at me as if to say *What is your problem, you sissy? Go on in there and find out what this is all about.* I don't know about you, but I believe dogs can say more with a slight twist of their eyebrow than most people can convey with a hundred words. We walked back down the front walk toward the street, but Dingo continued to look back. My hands were shaking as I pulled at her leash to lead her away from the house. Once safely on the street, I turned around and noticed the shade that had been partially open was now completely shut.

"That was friggin' freaky," I said aloud as I walked Dingo back toward our home. I wondered what I could have been thinking or imagining or . . . dreaming? Was I going crazy? Was this some sort of out-of-body thing? Or maybe it was just my idiot older brother messing with me. He did stupid tricks like that sometimes, but I knew he was at the office right then, so it couldn't be him. Nevertheless, I was pretty sure I wasn't dreaming, but I didn't understand any of this. I was scared, but my curiosity was greater than my fear. I would go back. I had to go back.

Chapter 4

DESPITE APPEARANCES TO THE CONTRARY, WE ALL HAVE SOMETHING WRONG WITH US

A friend of mine once told me that if everyone we knew met in a big circle, and we could see the problems that each person was dealing with at that time, no one would trade their problems for someone else's. For the most part, I think I believe that, but my problems were about to get a lot worse.

When Rachel arrived back at the house, Jessica and I were snuggling together on the couch. I heard the back-door slam and I could tell that it was the kind of slam that was done with the foot. And that usually meant that Rachel was carrying something heavy and didn't have a free hand. Now, I know that a good husband would rush to help his wife with whatever it was she was carrying, but I was so comfortable sitting there with my daughter. And I didn't want to lose the perfect snuggle position that Jessica and I had worked so hard to achieve.

"A little help here, Neil," Rachel barked from the kitchen as she dropped the two bags of groceries on the island counter.

I adjusted my sitting position nervously when Rachel peered into the room. Her jaw dropped when she saw Jessica.

"Neil! What the heck is she doing here?"

"The school called," I said as I pulled my arm up from behind Jessica and Dingo jumped down off the couch.

"What do you mean? Is she sick?" Rachel probed as she entered the room. "She doesn't look sick."

"I threw up, Mommy," Jessica said. Rachel knelt in front of her and placed her hand on Jessica's knee.

"I'm sorry, honey. Are you okay?" Rachel inquired tenderly.

"I'm okay now. Too many bacons. Daddy and I watch Junkies."

I sat up completely now as I knew I would have to go into a defensive posture to handle Rachel's oncoming attack about my choice of television show.

"Neil, what the heck?! You should have called me! I would have gotten her. She is my responsibility when it comes to things like this."

"I gave her some ice cream and she's okay," I said, trying to get the subject changed as quickly as possible. "I think she just ate too much bacon this morning. Right, Jessie?"

Rachel reached out and felt Jessica's forehead. "She seems okay. No fever."

I stood up as Rachel gently rubbed Jessica's stomach. It would be within minutes and I knew what was coming. It's not that my wife is mean. She is just a bit of a control freak and I knew that no matter what, I was going to get a battery of questions about when, where, why, and how I could possibly have decided that eating ice cream and watching a show about garbage-picking could be healthy for a sick seven-year-old.

"Okay, sweet Jessica. I'm glad you are feeling better," Rachel whispered softly to her. "Do you need anything? Do you want to lie down on your bed upstairs?"

"No, Mommy. I like it here. Can Daddy stay with me?"

As those words left Jessica's mouth, I knew that whatever trouble I was in before would now be magnified. You see, Rachel is an amazing mother, but she gets angry and hurt when the girls show their preference for me. Rachel literally thinks of everything and does all she can to give our children a full, well-rounded life. In addition to meals, laundry, homework, etc., she signs them up for classes, volunteers at their school, and basically thinks ahead of everything that they might need, want, or even think they might need or want. I, on the other hand, watch all this effort and supplement the kids with other things. Easier things. I know, it isn't fair, but I get to be the fun parent. When the essential important responsibilities of the day end, that is where I take over. Mostly, I play games or music or just hang out with my kids and that includes watching television. I have even acclimated to watching children's shows as the producers of these programs are smart and usually throw something in the program to hook the parents too. I marvel even today when I watch a Bugs Bunny cartoon as they are clearly created on two levels. One for the small child and another for the parent watching with the small child. I simply love cartoons.

Still, as much fun as we have, I see my fatherly role as having another very important component. I know Rachel believes in God, but she doesn't impart her beliefs on our children. Conversely, I am a minister's son, so I can't help but adopt some of the religious rituals we carried out when I was a child. As you might imagine, I was exposed to a steady dose of organized religion growing up, but to me it was just part of normal daily life. In addition to attending church and doing church activities, my parents made us pray before meals and bed and it became habitual and even rote. We knew the Lord's Prayer by heart as soon as we could talk, and I worked to make that a routine for my girls as well. It might all be just good mental psychology, like yoga or meditation, but I think it is important and it might be why the girls prefer me to Rachel when they are upset or not feeling well.

Most evenings and once the dishes are done, it is my job to calm the girls down and get them ready for bed. Once they settle into their rooms, I usually tell them a story (that I make up) and then we pray. After the Lord's Prayer, we pray for our immediate family and then we pay homage to some significant people that my girls have not and probably will never meet. My daughters, you see, are both adopted. They were each around eight months old when we brought them home from China (eighteen months apart), but they are just now starting to understand what it really means to be adopted. There is an unavoidable mental adjustment process for all adopted kids, and they will inevitably wonder why they were given up by their birth parents. Despite the hurt or pain they may feel, I want them to see this instead as a loving gesture by their birth parents. So we pray for what we call their "China parents" and I hope these two strangers in China are somehow comforted and aware that their baby is okay.

I was almost forty years old when we first decided to go the adoption route. My wife and I tried to have children on our own, but it just didn't work out. Like many couples today, we did in vitro procedures, shots, fertility pills, and even some other experimental stuff, but nothing worked. Yet, somewhere in the back of my mind, I knew we were still meant to have kids. And I wanted to adopt. Heck, I wanted to be adopted when I was a kid as I thought it made you seem "cool," like a vagabond in a Clint Eastwood western. The kids I knew who were adopted were happy and they seemed to be proud of it. And I figured it would be especially fun to adopt a child of a different race. I can't imagine loving a biological child any more or differently than I do my girls. Genetics are just cells and mine aren't all that good anyway. I was never much more than an average student, and I know there is a part of my wife's genetic history that contains a little insanity. Thus, not having to deal with our gene pool was a positive. People often ask if they are sisters and I think, *Duh*. I know what they mean, but I always respond, "Of course they are sisters." I realize that they are asking if they came from the same biological mother, which they didn't.

"Neil!" Rachel shouted out as she moved her way back toward the garage door. "Can you please help me with the groceries?"

"Sure. I'm coming," I replied as I kissed Jessica on the forehead. I looked lovingly at my daughter all curled up on the couch before I headed to the garage to face the music.

"What the heck were you thinking, Neil?" Rachel exclaimed as she grabbed the handle of a plastic bag and handed it to me. "Did you not even think to call me? Our baby is sick and that is my job."

"I knew you were busy and I didn't mind. And she seems okay, you know? I had it covered," I said confidently as I grabbed six plastic sacks at once to carry inside.

"Look. Just call me from now on. Okay? I'm sorry, but I just don't ... trust you."

Rachel knew very well that those words would sting, so I tried to restrain my instinctive reaction to argue with her. But try as I might, I couldn't resist.

"Why the heck don't you trust me? I did the same dang thing you would have done. And I was home when they called, and you weren't. What's the difference?"

"The difference," Rachel said as she stopped inside the doorway and changed into a whisper. "The difference is that I wouldn't have given her ice cream. The difference is that I would have called the doctor. The difference is that I would have gone back to her classroom to get her things. Do you even know if she has homework? "

I have learned over our seventeen years of marriage that this is a good point in our typical exchange to keep my mouth shut. It is far wiser to let Rachel get all her complaints about me out on the table before responding. It only adds to her frustration if I start my defense before she has finished her opening arguments.

"Now, I have to go back there. And letting her watch that stupid program, I told you a hundred times that *Junksters* is not age-appropriate material for either of our girls. Do you really want them to aspire to a life driving around the country and going through other people's garbage?"

I paused for a moment thinking that the garbage picking life actually sounded pretty cool. I hoped that she might be done with her rant, but I could tell from the body posture that she was just gathering steam.

"I leave the house for three hours and what have you done? Anything? Did you take out the recycling like I asked? Did you schedule the painters?" Rachel inquired before turning around to get another grocery sack. I kept silent knowing full well that I had not done either of those things.

"Are you going to answer me?" she demanded as she pushed the button to close the garage door.

It was time to respond.

"Um . . . no. I haven't called them yet. I'll do that this afternoon after my nap."

The word *nap* was still on my tongue when I knew that I could not suck it back into my mouth. It was a terrible mistake to have uttered that word. It was like lighting a dynamite fuse in Rachel's brain and I knew it.

"*Nap?* Boy, oh boy. I wish that I had time to take a nap. That sure would be nice, but if I did that, then the family wouldn't get any dinner. Would they? Would they, Neil?"

It has taken me my entire lifetime to figure out what a rhetorical question is. I'm still not totally sure, just like my continued confusion between an *analogy* and a *metaphor*. But, in this case, I knew that this was rhetorical and that I would be better off keeping my mouth shut.

"You beat everything. You know that?" Rachel continued. "It's like I have three children. But you are the worst of the three. I literally can't ask you to do anything."

After Rachel said this, I was dying to reply that she asked me to do things constantly. I just didn't do them.

She entered the kitchen and began putting things into the cabinets and refrigerator. I sat down at the kitchen table to resume my crossword puzzle.

"You could be helping me with this too, you know?" Rachel said, even though she knew I would only put things into the wrong place, which would create even more work for her. "I truly don't know what else I can do if you continually look at me like I am a witch for asking you to help around the house. But boy, oh boy, we don't want to interrupt your nap time, or your crossword puzzle, do we?"

Rhetorical again. For those who don't already know, I must say that "naps rock!" I love them, but my wife hated the fact that I took a nap virtually every day and at any time the mood hit me. My mind and body were used to it and many sleep specialists can verify that this practice is not only healthy, it is ultimately productive too. And besides, I usually only take a twenty to thirty-minute snooze. Still, the fact remains, I am addicted to naps and I can be a bear if I am forced to skip one. My wife's theory is that taking a nap during the day causes a person to need even more sleep at night. She might have a point as I have only seen the first ten minutes of almost every DVD brought into our home for "movie night." Once my head reclines in that leather easy chair, I know I'm not long for the world. And for some reason, that drives Rachel nuts, especially when I start to snore.

"Now I have to drive back to the school to get Jessie's stuff. Thanks a lot. I really needed that and I'm sure you aren't going to do it. You need your nap, right?"

Third time rhetorical.

"We can go out for dinner tonight. How about that? So you don't have to cook," I said, thinking this would be a good concession to start getting back in Rachel's good graces. Yet, my culinary bribes hardly ever worked, and she just wasn't ready to let me off the hook.

"I've already thawed the chicken. We are eating at home," she replied harshly as she went back into the garage.

I watched her as she took the last of the grocery bags out of the back of our SUV and I wondered if there was anything I could do to get her to feel better about me. But she knows my mind and she knows that no matter what I say, my real motivation is just to get her to leave me alone. Sadly, this is only one of the unfortunate things about the state of our marriage today. Our troubles can basically be boiled down to two primary categories: I want to be left alone, and she just doesn't like me that much anymore.

Chapter 5

DREAMS ALWAYS MEAN SOMETHING

I dreamed last night that I was at the top of a skyscraper as it began to shake and lean. I looked out the window and realized that there was a massive storm hitting the building and it was rocking the structure dangerously. It couldn't have been more than a minute before the inevitable happened. The building started to crumble, and I knew, at that moment, that I was going to die. I was alone on the forty-seventh floor of this building as it started to fall toward the ground. The building was collapsing on itself much like the World Trade Center towers, and I knew that I would eventually be crushed to death and buried beneath tons and tons of rubble. I said only one thing as I descended to the ground. It was *"I'm not ready, God."* I was expecting a painful crushing of flesh and bones, but that didn't happen. Everything just went totally black and there was no sound at all. I knew I wasn't dead, but I wasn't alive either. It was just me and God, but God was everywhere, and I was nothing. I don't think I have ever been so frightened, but fortunately I woke up and realized it was only a dream. I was relieved, but I also knew it had to mean something. All dreams do, right?

When Dingo and her wagging tail came to the bed to greet me that morning, I knew that this day was going to be something different. Didn't Bruce Springsteen sing "If you die in your dreams, you really die in your bed"? Why, then, was I alive? What was the significance of that dream? I knew it was not any ordinary dream. God was sending me a message and I was determined to explore the meaning of what I had experienced in my sleep. And I knew instinctively that the green-door house had something to do with it.

"Come on, Dingo. Let's go," I mumbled as I slid out of bed.

I put on my Cleveland Cavaliers sweatshirt and slipped on my blue Crocs to get Dingo outside as quickly as I could. (Yes, despite protests from my family and friends, I am a huge fan of Crocs: easily the most comfortable and practical shoes ever made.) Dingo and I were both aware that we were on a mission today. She did her business quickly this morning as we headed straight for the house. It was not fully light outside, but it was bright enough to see inside the window and down the narrow hallway. Everything was much like it had been before, but this time one of the doors in the hallway was open. I nervously reached down to touch the doorknob and it seemed as if the door opened on its own. This time I was committed to go further and prove to myself that I was not a chicken or crazy despite feeling a little of both. I stepped cautiously into the house and entered the front hall. The wood beneath my feet felt a bit un-sturdy and I felt a shiver run down my spine. Dingo trailed slightly behind me and then the door closed on its own behind us.

"Anybody home?" I called out.

Dingo wagged her tail and looked up at me as if to say, *Don't you see him?*

I walked further into the hallway and let the leash fall to the floor. Dingo immediately took advantage of her freedom and trotted happily into the adjacent room. I followed her slowly and saw a dusty brown couch in the far corner and a single red ladder-back chair in front of the window. Dingo barked for some reason which startled me, and I considered making a dash toward the door. But then, I heard a deep voice. It was the same voice I had heard in my head a few days earlier.

"Come on in, Neil, and have a seat."

I looked around the room and Dingo seemed to be looking directly at something as she moved closer to the couch. Her tail was wagging happily. I blinked and rubbed my eyes a few times and gradually a solitary male figure appeared standing just a few feet away from me. He was a youthful man in his mid-twenties with a head of sandy brown hair. He had a pale complexion and was dressed in a brown suit with a white shirt with thin green pinstripes. His tie was brown and green, and his shoes were those old-fashioned two-toned types, like from the Roaring Twenties. He motioned me over to the couch and I moved in that direction as he patted Dingo on the head.

"Hello again. I'm Dobie," the voice said. "Come on in and have a seat."

The shadows from the windowpane hit the couch precisely where he motioned me to sit. I sat down nervously at the other end of the couch as the glare of the early morning sun shone on my face. I shielded my eyes and picked up the leash to pull Dingo over toward me for comfort.

"I'm your guide today. Now, if you are ready, I will explain what this house is all about."

The mysterious man paced in front of the couch, which occasionally kept the sun out of my eyes. It also created a halo effect around him that made his body look like it was glowing.

"I know this must be a bit strange for you, but I assure you, this is really happening, and you are completely safe."

For some odd reason, I felt a lot less safe as soon as he said that. Whenever anyone tells me that there is nothing to worry about, I know it is time to start worrying. My mind momentarily flashed to an image of me being emaciated and locked in chains in a dungeon, but I quickly shook off that image. Dobie then sat on the other end of the couch and leaned forward towards me. His calm, pleasant expression comforted me a bit.

"So, uh, who are you?" I asked with trepidation.

"I'm your . . . guide. I'm here to . . . well, how do I say this?" Dobie responded as he crossed and uncrossed his legs. When he did, I noticed that the leather on his shoes was old and wrinkled, but the soles were still in relatively good shape. "I'm here to help you on your journey."

"What journey?" I inquired.

"It's like this," he said softly. "You have been given a unique opportunity to look back on your life. And I'm here to show you how it's done. To help you."

"How? What do you mean?" I asked, still feeling emotionally unsure of myself.

"This house. It is a special place that will allow you to go back in time. Well, we don't send you back in time really, because you can't change what you have already lived, you know that . . . but we can allow you to relive it or live the experience again, and maybe this time you will see it from a different perspective. Do you see?"

"No. I don't," I muttered.

Dobie must have comprehended the utter confusion on my face.

"Let me try this again. I always have trouble explaining this part, but it is . . . well, it's hard to explain until you actually . . . do it. You know?"

"Listen," I responded. "I don't know who you are or what all this is, but, well... are you sure you aren't a psycho nut job?"

Dobie got up and paced back and forth in front of the window again, carefully stepping around Dingo each time he passed.

"I wish this was easier to explain, but then again if it was easy, it wouldn't be as effective . . . or at least we hope it is effective. Whether it is or not is really up to you."

"Wait. Are you like a guardian angel kind of thing? Like in that movie, the Christmas one with Jimmy Stewart. You're Clarence the angel, right?"

"No. I'm not an angel and my name is not Clarence. It's Dobie. Like I said. I'm more like a guide. I'm here to help you with the process."

"Okay," I said, feeling slightly more confident now. "Let me see if I got this. Your name is Dobie and you are my guide for going back in time? To go back and live my life over again?"

"No. Well, yes, it is something like that, but not exactly. Like I said, you will get a better idea once we get started."

"Get started with what?" I asked as Dobie stopped pacing and looked directly into my eyes.

"I thought we would start with a time from your childhood," he responded. "You can pick the experience or the day. Just think of an event you would like to revisit and we can go there. We can go back in time."

Go back in time? What the heck was this? I thought I must be dreaming again, but this did not have that dream quality. No, this was real, but how could it be? Who was this guy, Dobie? What kind of ridiculous name was that anyway? Could I really go back in time? This was all a little too much for me to take in.

"Neil, are you okay?" Dobie asked.

"Um . . ." I replied, snapping out of my semi-stupor.

"Are you ready to get started?" he inquired again.

"Um, give me a minute," I replied.

As best as I could understand, I was supposed to pick a time from my childhood to relive? Sadly, I don't remember a lot of my childhood that clearly anymore, and the parts I do remember are mostly . . . bad. Then, without even realizing it, I blurted out these words.

"Sixth grade."

"Ah, yes." Dobie nodded. "Sixth grade. The music class."

I pondered how he could have known that the music class was what I meant and then I wondered why the heck I would ever want to go back to that day. That horrible, horrible day.

"Yes. Music class, but . . . how did you know?" I inquired.

"I've been studying up on you. You consider this to be a defining moment in your life, don't you?"

"I hope not. It was a . . . total disaster. Heck. I passed out. In front of . . . the entire class."

Dobie nodded.

"I was so . . . I was so embarrassed." I uttered while shaking my head. "I looked like an idiot."

Dobie was right actually. That day was a defining moment for me, but in a bad way.

"I'd love to do that day over again," I said emphatically. "Yeah, I would do it differently. First, I wouldn't volunteer to sing in that stupid musical. Second, I wouldn't let everyone see me collapse and faint from fear. Maybe a lot of things will turn out better for me if I could get that day back and change it."

"No, no, no," Dobie said, shaking his head. "It doesn't work like that. You can't change what happened, Neil. You can only relive the experience."

"Relive it? You mean it all happens the same as before? What the heck good is that?" I replied indignantly.

"I think you need to try it and then maybe it will make more sense. Come on. Let's go. Follow me."

Dobie proceeded to walk slowly down the hallway. Dingo followed closely behind Dobie and they continued to the one door that was slightly open. I noticed the broken door handle that was still sitting on the floor in front of one of the closed doors.

"What's behind that door?" I asked as we proceeded.

"Not that one. Not for today anyway. This other door will take you where you want to go," Dobie said as he opened the door further down more completely and motioned for me to enter.

Dingo sat down next to Dobie and seemed to be motioning for me to get moving too. And with that, I entered the door which led to some descending stairs. Taking a deep breath, I stepped down onto the first step and then began my first ever trip back in time.

Chapter 6

MEMORIES REMAIN LOCKED IN OUR MINDS FOREVER

Even from my earliest memories, my father was a very intimidating figure. First, he was very tall (6'4") and big (230 pounds). He had a large head with sharp facial features and jet-black hair. He rarely smiled, which always bothered me, but that was just who he was. Like Rachel, things also just weren't ever that funny to him. He seemed to be an apathetic person in general, but it was clear to almost everyone that he was a natural-born leader. People simply admired my father before he even opened his mouth. And when he did speak, it was likely to be short and carefully targeted. So much for genetics as I am in so many ways the opposite of him. As a kid, I was short for my age and I talked way too much. I was always getting in trouble for running my mouth in class and I was much more of a follower than a leader. As my father would often say, "Neil was the guy who would jump off the bridge if everyone else was doing it." He was right. I generally went with the crowd, so I'm lucky they didn't jump off that proverbial bridge. I would have done it for sure. I wanted to be liked and I wasn't sure if my own father liked me, much less my peers.

So, when I descended those creaky stairs that day, it was as if I had erased thirty-plus years of dealing with my feelings of inadequacy. With each step, I could sense my body changing, and then hair was suddenly covering my entire head again for the first time in years. As my eyes adjusted to the darkness, I could see that my hands were thinner and more youthful. And then, there I was, eleven years old again and sitting in the auditorium of my old elementary school. My music teacher, Mrs. McFadden, was sitting at the piano adjusting the sheet music in front of her. She was a middle-aged woman with long straight auburn hair and she wore ridiculously large red glasses. When I looked around the room at my classmates, their names all jumped back into my mind.

My recollection of this period in my life was now crystal clear. It was as if the images had touched off a spark in my brain and all the thoughts of that day came flooding back into my mind. I had no trouble remembering the music we were practicing. It was Andrew Lloyd Weber's *Joseph and the Amazing Technicolor Dreamcoat*. I loved the songs from that musical and still listen to them today. As Mrs. McFadden looked up from the piano, I remembered the terrified feeling I had whenever she asked me to sing something. I knew I had a decent voice, but I did not have any experience singing in front of others on my own. Being an alto in the church choir helped me develop a basic understanding of music and harmony. I didn't study it like a profession, but I did have a good ear for it and that is why I initially volunteered to be in the musical.

I stood on the back of the podium next to my peers and everything was just as Dobie had suggested. I couldn't change anything from what I had previously done. I was there inside my body in that class again, but my impulse control was gone. It was quite strange, and it felt like I was in a movie, but the movie images were coming out of my eyes and projecting into the room. I couldn't alter my motions or impact anything. I could only observe the situation as if the current, fifty-year-old version of me was trapped inside the body of this younger version of myself. I remembered what I had long thought about time travel. Even though it was great drama, the concept simply was not possible. Even my favorite time travel movies, *The Time Machine*, *Back to the Future*, and *Peggy Sue Got Married* were great entertainment, but I would always catch something about the concept that didn't work or was simply not feasible. So how could this be happening to me now and, more importantly, why? Were the brain cells that contained this

THE HOUSE *of* REMEMBER WHEN

information simply being recalled as I looked about the classroom? Why couldn't I change the outcome from that same day thirty-nine years ago? While I was pondering all this, the once very familiar and shrill voice of Mrs. McFadden rang out.

"Mr. Moreland, can you please pay attention? This is your part and I want you to emote with confidence. You need to sing louder and project your voice out into the entire auditorium. Come on now. Project!" *Project* was Mrs. McFadden's favorite word and she used it a lot. To this day, I hate hearing that term as it always brings me back to that depressing day. And besides, I didn't really know what she meant by it. Was I supposed to throw my voice out there somehow? Emote confidently? What the heck was that!? I was totally perplexed so I just looked up and smiled nervously. And then I felt a rush of embarrassment come over my face.

"I need you to lift your head and sing loudly to me. Come on now! Look straight at me and let me hear you."

Mrs. McFadden played a single note on her piano and it echoed out into the large auditorium. One of my worst memories of that year was when Mrs. McFadden would ask us to sing our own name at the beginning of class. She called it a warming-up exercise and we all hated it. I hated it especially as it not only didn't help me warm up; it made me think that my name was stupid. Neil Moreland. It was such a plain name, and I wasn't even a Cornelius. It was simply Neil. I often wished my parents had come up with something more creative. Even my middle name, James, held no appeal for me. No, mine was the type of name that emerged when your parents couldn't agree on anything. I had always wished my name was something like Levon or Clint or something really cool like Deacon.

"Please project your voice, Mr. Moreland. Loud and clear so we can all hear it. Don't keep us all waiting," Mrs. McFadden stated again, but this time more emphatically.

This was the moment, the horror I had felt so many years ago. The embarrassment of

fainting in front of everyone. How stupid I must be looking again. I looked around at my classmates who seemed to be as scared as me, and then I felt the blood rushing out of my face. The weakness in your body that foreshadows the loss of consciousness hit me, and I knew that it was coming. And then it happened. I blacked out and fell backward off the short podium. And for the next few minutes or maybe more, I was unconscious.

The first time I lived through this, I was so embarrassed that I couldn't bear to go to school the next day. I heard later that many in the room thought I was faking it when it happened and that I was trying to get a good laugh out of the class. I let them think that. Why not? It was better than the truth that I was simply a big giant "chicken" who passed out from embarrassment. When I did faint, I was in total darkness, which seemed appropriate as I was reliving the darkest hour of my childhood.

I came back to consciousness a few minutes later and there I was again on the floor with the middle-school principal fanning me with a magazine.

"What happened, Neil?" he asked as I tried to sit up. The principal gently placed my head back down onto a seat cushion someone had placed there.

"I don't know," I said groggily.

"You must be sick," the principal said in a soft tone. "Do you have the flu?"

"Maybe. Yeah. That could be it," I said in response knowing full well that I was not sick at all. All I knew was that at least fifteen other kids from that class were now laughing at me. How ridiculous that I would have fainted over something so insignificant. It wasn't even the full production. It was just a small rehearsal. As Charlie Brown would often say whenever he failed at something: "Good grief!" And in those days, I felt very much like Charlie Brown. I was the guy who wanted to be more than he was. And on that day, I wasn't even as good as Charlie Brown.

It was weeks before I could go an hour without having a flashback to the horror of fainting in front of my peers. It was literally years before I didn't think of that event at least once a day, and I still think about it often. It was a pivotal moment as it defined me as a person with a weak constitution. This was not at all who I wanted to be, but from that moment on, I would dread crowds and do my best to avoid any public speaking opportunity. I would also avoid being in the spotlight in any sport or situation. I never ran for school government. I never was the quarterback or the star pitcher. I was a follower in every sense of the word. And from that moment on, and despite a relatively good singing voice, I abandoned any idea of being a performer. All I could do was imagine fainting in front of hundreds of people. What if it was caught on camera and millions saw it happen? I'd be the poster-child of *America's Stupidest Home Videos*. Today it would be over a trillion YouTube hits.

This irrational fear eventually became a phobia of sorts and, in early adulthood, I even sought counseling to help me with my nervousness. Like a lot of phobias, it progressed over time to where I would start sweating at even the slightest thought of people paying too much attention to me. Little did I realize that one moment in time could dramatically change the entire course of my life. When I met with the psychologist, I told him that I went from an eleven-year-old child thinking I could do almost anything to a chronically insecure person who avoided any situation that could expose me to more ridicule. The impact of that event was huge, and here I was reliving it again. Why? Again, what was the point if I couldn't change it?

There was silence in the room as my eleven-year-old self finally found the strength to sit up. Mrs. McFadden and her obnoxious glasses were nowhere in sight, but the principal was looking down on me with what seemed like genuine compassion. He held my arm gently as I straightened myself up to look around the room. Not a single soul was laughing. Funny, but I hadn't remembered it that way. My classmates actually appeared sincerely relieved as my face gradually regained a normal color. A few of them even offered to help me up and walk with me to the door. Hmmm . . .

Okay, so I had relived this event. But why? For what purpose? As Dobie said, I could not change the event. There was nothing I could do except remember the entire ordeal. I felt intense anger with the music teacher for not recognizing what this event did to me. Where was she in my darkest hour? I was only eleven for Pete's sake. Couldn't she have taken me under her wing and worked with me to get over my stage fright? I dropped out of the production, of course, and she never even asked me why. Come to think of it, I don't think I ever saw her again. That turned out to be my last thought before I found myself on the couch in the front room of the green-doored house. Dobie sat next to me as I rubbed my eyes to try to clear the blur in my brain.

"Well, that was fun," I said sarcastically. "I wonder what grand memories await me behind door number three."

"Pretty brutal, huh?" Dobie said empathetically.

"One of the worst moments of my life. What possible good did it do me to relive that?"

Dobie stood and faced me as I looked around the room to see Dingo curled up and asleep in the corner.

"Did you notice anything different this time?" Dobie asked.

I leaned my head back against the couch and closed my eyes to think. As I did, the images of the concerned faces of my classmates came shooting into my mind. But even so, it all still seemed to be a disaster.

"No, I don't think so," I replied.

"But you do know. What was different?" Dobie asked as if he already knew the answer.

"I guess. I guess . . . I didn't hear any laughing."

"Okay, and then what?" Dobie inquired.

"And then I . . . heck, I fainted. I hit the floor. Plop. Like a friggin' dope."

"Who says you looked like a dope? Did anyone say that to you? Maybe you had a bad breakfast or were not feeling well. Did you ever consider that?"

"Heck no," I replied. "Even if I had eaten dog food for breakfast, I mean, who does that? Who faints in a stupid sixth grade music class? I wasn't even on the main stage. It ruined me for performing, forever. I couldn't even go on with an insignificant middle-school play. I had to quit. What if I had fainted in front of a full auditorium?"

Dobie began pacing the room again as if he was in deep thought.

"There must be a reason we are starting with this event. I think this was a big part of your life and it is worth exploring further."

"I think it is worth forgetting. They may not have laughed right then, but they probably still think about it today and laugh when they think of me. And my asshole teacher did nothing to help."

"Maybe the teacher was embarrassed for pushing you so hard. Maybe she felt like she was to blame and she was embarrassed too."

"Yeah, right. She didn't even come talk to me about it. It took me years to get over it. Why relive it now? If that is what this house is all about, I'm getting out of here," I said as I grabbed Dingo's leash.

"Wait, don't leave. Where are you going?"

I slammed the door on my way out, but I knew Dobie was right. Here I was, fifty years old and I still wasn't over this one event from my childhood. And yet, this time I did sense something different. The principal was nice to me. And I could see and sense the compassion on the faces of the others in the room.

My anger gradually subsided as I walked home. Dobie was right. I was starting to feel differently about that day and decided that it would be worthwhile to return to the house for another trip as soon as I was recovered from this one.

Chapter 7

I AM A LOT LIKE HOWARD HUGHES

It's not just me. I think we are all a little bit like Howard Hughes. If you know about his life, you can't help but be envious of his early years. It seemed he had everything. Good looks. Inherited millions. Women. Good looks . . . and *women*. And it seemed he could have anything else he wanted too. The sky was literally his limit! From every starlet in Hollywood to as many planes, cars, homes, and hotels as you could ever imagine owning. He was at one time, one of the richest people on the planet. He took huge risks with his fortune (e.g., the *Spruce Goose*), but he always seemed to end up better off and richer than before. He was once lucky enough to survive a horrible plane crash that disfigured his face, but he simply grew a mustache to hide the scars. And it worked. Well, it certainly didn't stop him from attracting beautiful women. Yet, I read that even in those early years, he was not a happy person. His phobia of germs and eventually everything else gradually overtook his life. He reportedly died insane, weighing only ninety pounds with fingernails six inches long. How tragic. This man, more than any other I knew of, had everything, but he let his mind destroy it all. If you look at his entire life, I don't think anyone would trade their life for his. I know I wouldn't, but I also know that my mind had a way of destroying things too. Just like Howard Hughes.

My older brother's name is Theodore Charles Moreland Jr., but I call him Chuck. I think I am the only one that calls him that anymore as he usually insists that people call him Ted, like my father. I started calling him Chuck as soon as I could talk, but no one remembers exactly why. I know it is a nickname for Charles, but I think I called him that because it was easier for me to say than *Teddy*. My parents and most of his good friends call him Teddy, but for me, he was always going to be Chuck. At one point, I tried calling him "the Beaver" (like in the *Leave It to Beaver* television show), but he beat the crap out of me and warned me never to utter that nickname again. Nevertheless, he is my best friend and has been my entire life. We even went to the same college, so we could continue to hang out together. But unlike Ward and June, my father and mother pretty much ignored us and essentially, that meant we could run throughout the neighborhood like wild wolves.

My parents were polite and socially appropriate people, but extremely naïve as parents. They had no idea what we were doing when we were out of the house. From playing in the sewers to building forts with the neighbor's garbage cans, we did pretty much whatever we wanted. This naivete also enabled Chuck and me to do entirely inappropriate things. For example, I once paid a kid on the elementary school playground fifty cents for a picture of a naked girl. I raced home to show Chuck and he gave me fifty cents more to get another picture for him. The second picture was even racier than the first, and we displayed those pictures proudly on the closet doors in our room. We each printed our names in crayon above the girls' heads to denote whose girl was whose. I wasn't there to see my mother's expression when she came in to make the beds, but I can only imagine the horror she felt.

Being minister's kids also came with a certain amount of social scrutiny and pressure. The high expectation, you see, was on my father as the congregation saw us as extensions of his character. In our early childhood, we lived in an integrated neighbor and directly next door to an African American family. I don't think I ever thought a thing about the color of skin back then, but it was a time when race relations were very tense all over the country. The neighbors had kids a few years younger than us and we were still at that age when "younger" meant "not cool." It's not that they were bad kids; we just preferred playing with kids closer to our own ages. Still, sometimes, pure boredom led us to including them in whatever it was we were doing, and one day Chuck and I were attempting to play some sort of made-up outdoor game and they were involved. The game was a running game where the victim (randomly chosen) would be chased around trees, rocks, fences, and other obstacles, and then pummeled into oblivion once we caught up with him. So I guess it was a form of the simple game "chase" with a "smear the queer" element at the end.

Well, these kids were probably only four and five when Chuck and I were six and seven and that meant trouble. As expected, Chuck and I completely dominated the game and often celebrated demonstrably whenever we would catch them. Our big mouths and bullying once led to them calling us what we felt was a racial slur; they called us "white patties." I can admit to you today that I have no idea what a "white patty" is, but I knew our skin was white and that must have been the reason they called us that. It was Louisville in the late 1960s, and I hope you can believe me that I held no racist beliefs at that time or since. People are people to me, and they always have been, but these kids were calling us "white patties" and in response, my brother and I used the only comparative term we could think of. We called them "coloreds". It was not that I thought this was the right word to use in defending our honor against their viciously racially intoned "white patty" (read sarcasm here), but it was the only word we could come up with that seemed to be in the same category. Plus, we once had heard a distant relative use the term and my mother chastised him so fiercely, we knew it had to be a good word to use in retaliation for white patty.

It was less than fifteen minutes after our playing ended when the mother of the young boys came to our front door and rang the bell. My mother answered and was her normally friendly self when inviting the woman in the house.

"Oh, hello, Ellen. You are Ellen Sharpe, right? Please do come in."

Mrs. Sharpe came into the house and made a visual inspection of the living room.

"It is so nice to see you. May I do something for you, Mrs. Sharpe? Would you like some coffee?" my mother inquired while wiping her hands off on her apron.

"Yes. Yes, you can do something for me," Mrs. Sharpe began. "You can begin by telling me what kind of trash you are teaching your children."

"Why, you . . . what on earth do you mean?"

"Your kids, those boys, this is an integrated neighborhood, Mrs. Moreland. If you don't like it, then you should move."

"What? What are you saying? My boys? I mean. It's . . . we love, uh, we love it here," my mother responded.

"Well, your kids . . . they . . . well, they don't seem to agree."

My mother took off her apron and again motioned for Mrs. Sharpe to sit down on the sofa.

"Can I please get you some something to drink? Tea maybe? Please sit down. We can discuss this."

"I don't want to discuss it," Mrs. Sharpe replied sharply, continuing to stand. "I want to know what you plan to do about it. I know the kids don't learn trash like that down at the elementary school."

"Trash like what?" my mother said with growing trepidation. My mother was no dummy. She had a good sense of what was coming.

"Your boys. Those boys of yours. They called my sons____"

"Ahhh, nooo!" My mother swooned and looked as if she were about to collapse.

"Yes, they did," Mrs. Sharpe continued. "You can ask them. They'll tell you. And they must have learned it from . . . well, they didn't get it from the school. Not our school. Maybe you and your husband are okay with that kind of trash talk, but I assure you, it won't be accepted around here."

One note: My father had once been at a church hall where they had two separate water fountains. One had a sign that read "Whites Only" and the other read "Colored". My father had both signs and the water fountains torn down. He was disgusted as he should have been.

My mother quickly regained her composure and again motioned for Mrs. Sharpe to sit, which she finally did.

"Mrs. Sharpe, I assure you, my boys did not get that from me or my husband. Please believe me. You know my husband is the pastor at the Episcopal Church on Fourteenth Street. And our parish has many black families. Please don't think we are prejudiced. You just can't. Please don't think that."

As my mother implored Mrs. Sharpe to believe her, it was interesting to note that she did not defend us in any way. She knew it had to be true and believed it on the spot. Later that night, when my father learned of the incident, he was so angry he did what he always did when he was that mad: he ignored us. Believe me. There is no greater punishment for a seven- and six-year-old kid than being given the silent treatment by their father. I would have rather he had beat us silly with a paddle. And in this case, the treatment went on for weeks. My father (without giving away our identities) even preached about using racially charged words like that. We were clearly in the wrong, and while I still don't know what a "white patty" is, I do know it is nothing like using the word "colored". And I have never said the word or even written it since that day. But Chuck and I remember the experience and continue to regret it to this day. Or at least I do. I was especially sorry for hurting my parents so much.

It was the Saturday following my initial time-travel experience when Chuck stopped by my house to say hello to the girls and mooch some food from our kitchen.

"Yo, bro! Don't you guys have any peanuts or something salty?" Chuck asked as he foraged through our cabinets. "I need some protein. What about these cheese and peanut butter crackers? Can I have these?"

"Buy your own food, cheap ass," I responded.

Chuck pulled a bag of organic chips down from the upper shelf and I watched as he shoved a handful into his mouth.

"Hey, Chuck?" I asked in a manner that Chuck knew was not going to be good.

"What?" he mumbled through a mouthful of potato chips.

"Come here. I need to ask you something."

"Oh shit. What now?" Chuck said as he slowly meandered over to the couch where I was sitting. "You better not want to borrow any money."

I moved over to allow Chuck plenty of space to sit down on the end of the couch opposite me.

"Okay, here it is. If you could go back in time, I mean, if you could relive a part of your life, would you? I mean, if you could, where would you go? What would you want to see? If you could, I mean?"

Even though Chuck is fourteen months older than me, I am the one who appears to others to be the older brother. Chuck often acts years younger than his age (fifty-two) and with his divorce, he is now dating women ten to twenty years younger than him or more. But as I aged into my forties, my hair began to thin and somehow Chuck's hair seemed to get thicker. He doesn't admit it, but I think he may have done that hair club thing, but I am afraid to ask him. He cares about how he looks and I don't. As brothers and good friends, we used to get compared all the time and I will concede now that he is the better-looking one. He is in better shape and keeps his weight down. I have long given up being a skinny person. God just didn't make me that way and even when I do get skinny, I can't stay there. So, like Elvis in his later years, I have resigned to being twenty pounds too heavy. At this weight, I certainly don't have to turn down a good dessert when it is offered to me. I eat what I want, and I can still fit into my thirty-six jeans—most of the time—so I'm good with it.

"Why would you ask me that? What is going on with you?" Chuck asked as if he were genuinely concerned, which was not likely to be true.

"I'm just asking."

I felt awkward and oddly nervous, which I never am around Chuck. But I was about to tell him something that I knew sounded crazy.

"You see . . . I, uh, I just had this experience . . . it was a dream, I guess. And it got me wondering what it would be like if you could go back and see parts of your life again. Except you are really there in the moment; not just watching it, but actually reliving it."

"Where do you get these moronic ideas?" Chuck inquired with an awkward expression.

"I'm just asking. If there was a house on your street, and in this house, there were doors and each door led to another part of your life, and when you go down the stairs, you are there. In that past part of your life. And you can relive it."

I knew I was now at the edge of Chuck's comfort zone, but I continued.

"I mean, where would you go? What would you do if you could do that? Go back in time?"

"You should have been a fucking writer, you know that?" Chuck laughed. "With all that crazy shit in your head, why don't you put these neurotic ideas to good use and write a movie or something?"

This was as close to a compliment as I ever got from Chuck. And he was right. I always wanted to be a writer, but as a kid I also wanted to write songs and that seemed way cooler at the time. And despite my efforts to become the next James Taylor, no one ever told me that they thought I had that kind of talent. And then there was the performance anxiety which led me to keeping my songs pretty much to myself. So, I reluctantly gave up on that dream. The movie thing might still be possible, but it would be tough to fit in the writing with my job duties and my naps, of course.

"So, where would you go?" I asked again as Chuck stuffed another handful of chips into his mouth.

"Let's see. If I could go back..." he said whimsically while chewing. "Hmmm... I would go back to college, I think. Sophomore year. Yeah, sophomore year. I would go back and have another go with that Marjory Miller. Remember her? She was so friggin' hot."

I remembered Marjory. I knew her pretty well actually as she didn't mind when I hung around the two of them on campus. I even joined them on a lot of their dates, and I think we all enjoyed being with each other. I was a good straight man for Chuck and his immature humor, and Marjory did laugh at most of his stupid stories. She liked Chuck a lot back then, but Chuck was a fraternity guy and she couldn't stand the shenanigans that went on in that frat house. After she had her fill of Chuck drinking himself silly at keg parties, she dumped him, and Chuck was devastated. Marjory called me later to explain her reasoning for the breakup, which I found a little odd. Why was she calling me? I liked Marjory and she was easy to talk to. But she was off-limits because of Chuck, even if she did have one very hot body.

"Marjory was sweet-looking," I said to Chuck as innocently as possible.

"I had that going for a couple of months, but she gave me the heave after I threw up on her dress at the sock-hop dance. She was great in the sack, though. Wow, I would definitely want to do that again."

"Hmmm. That is actually a great idea."

"What?" Chuck replied curiously. "You would want to do her too?"

"No, not Marjory. Do you remember Cindy Wintergreen?" I asked.

"Sure, I do," Chuck countered. "She was in my class and she was smokin', man. Great rack. Great ass. But I'll bet you she is two hundred pounds now. Hot girls like that always get fat. That's just how it works."

"That's not at all what happens, you idiot," I said confidently. "Fat girls get fatter and hot girls stay hot until they turn fifty. And then nobody is hot after fifty. That's when the nicer fat girls start looking good."

We laughed as I checked around the family room area to make sure my girls and my wife were nowhere close enough to hear any of this.

"Cindy was cute, man. But I bet you she got fat. That's all I'm saying. Did you ever see her mom at the pool? That old lady's droopy boobs sagged like two coconuts in a plastic shopping bag."

Chuck lifted the bag of chips and poured the remainder into his mouth while my mind raced with thoughts of Cindy Wintergreen. She was my first true sexual experience, and I think I was her first too. I remembered it so clearly. Or at least I thought I did. We did it in her house one summer weekend after my junior year of high school while her parents were out of town. She was an aggressive girl and I was so nervous around her at school that I could hardly speak to her. Her confidence quite frankly intimidated me, but people told me that she liked me, and I assumed it had to be true. I once reasoned that she liked me because I was one of the few white guys in our high school that wasn't Jewish. Cindy was Jewish, but for some reason she never dated Jewish guys. I don't know if it was a rebellion thing or what, but I didn't consider that too much back then. For some odd reason, she liked me. She asked me to come over to her house and I thought that this night could be *the* night, if you know what I mean.

I was just about to start giving Chuck more details when Rachel walked into the room.

"Oh hi, honey" I said a bit uncomfortably. Rachel had a way of knowing whenever I was talking or even thinking about the wrong thing. And she knew immediately that Chuck and I were talking trashy guy stuff.

"Hello, Chuck. How are things?" Rachel queried as she set down the laundry basket on the card table. "How are the boys doing? I heard Maggie made the varsity soccer team."

Rachel asked all this because the kids had recently moved back in with Chuck. His wife had kept his children the first three years after the breakup, but she wanted to do some traveling with her new job and Chuck got them back. He had twin fourteen-year-old boys and a sixteen-year-old daughter. His two boys were even wilder than we were as kids. Don't get me wrong, I love his kids. And Chuck's kids are relatively good, but they are a bit rude and simply have no clue how to act around adults. They expect things that we would have never gotten as kids. I used to ask Chuck why he didn't discipline them more and he had no good answer. He either didn't care or didn't have the skills to do it. I remember one Thanksgiving holiday at my parents' house and one meal in particular. His boys were about nine at the time.

"I'm going to go play Nintendo!" Chuck's son Todd shouted out to him as my mother placed side dishes on the table for our holiday meal. His other son, Ben, had eaten three rolls already, but my mother had not yet sat down.

"I'm going too," Ben said matter-of-factly. "I don't like this food anyway."

I sat there in amazement as Chuck nodded in agreement that they could leave the table. When we were kids, my father would have never let that happen. Being rude or disrespecting my mother (in front of my Dad) was not tolerated in his house.

"What are you doing?" I asked Chuck in utter amazement.

"It's not worth the fight, bro," Chuck responded. "They get their way in the end anyway."

After staring at Chuck in disbelief for a few moments, I decided I couldn't let it go.

"Dad would have murdered us," I uttered under my breath, so my father wouldn't hear. And Chuck knew that was true. In our childhood days, it was still acceptable to spank a child as long as it was in a controlled fashion (like with a paddle). Times have changed, that's for sure. I would never dream of spanking one of my kids. But I don't deny that Chuck and I needed to be paddled and paddled often. We had rules in our house and swat values corresponding to different infractions. For example, saying "shut-up" or "pig" to each other was worth one swat. Saying shut-up to my mother was five swats. Saying "shut-up" to my father... well, it would likely have meant death via paddling. My mother kept track of the (paddle) swats on a chalkboard in the kitchen. When my father would get home, he would note the tallies and we would prepare ourselves for the corporal punishment that was very deserved.

But Chuck was right. In the end, his boys pretty much did what they wanted, and we pretended not to notice. His children were the unfortunate product of a painful divorce, and I understand that the separated parents sometimes overcompensate from feeling guilty. His kids would never have a normal family life again, and I felt for them. Even though my folks weren't the perfect role model parents, they sure did love each other. As a couple, they seemed to be symbiotic. We never questioned their loyalty to each other, and they never contradicted each other when it came to discipline or granting permission. If my father said no, then my mother said no. They were united, and we knew it. Rachel and I did not have that going for us, and that worried me for managing the years ahead. I know unity is important.

Still, I feel sorry for Chuck. He is a neat freak and likes a tidy and clean house. But these days, his modern bi-level home looks more like a GI Joe, rat-infested combat zone. He even has a cleaning person come in twice a week, but you would never know it unless you got there within a few minutes of her leaving the house. His kids run all over the place like wild animals, and I'm sure that was part of the reason that he and his wife didn't make it. From the couples I have witnessed, when the kids start to rule the house, the marriage is less likely to succeed. In our home, Rachel kept things so neat and orderly that I feared not putting a book back in the exact spot I found it. There was a place for everything, and it was our job to find that place. Rachel was so strict, in fact, that an hour of play consisted of ten minutes of organizing, twenty minutes of playing, and then thirty minutes of cleaning up and getting everything back into the proper cabinet or drawer. For us (me and the girls), it was often far easier and much more relaxing to watch television.

"Don't mind me, boys," Rachel said as she picked up the laundry basket to leave. "You can go back to talking about your old girlfriends now. I'm heading out to yoga."

She knew. Somehow, she always knew.

"Neil don't forget, you have to take the girls to a birthday party at three. They're up playing in their rooms now. Don't forget, okay? Make sure Mary wears that blue dress I put on her bed. Don't let Jessica wear those horrible green pants. They are filthy. I put an outfit out for her too. The directions and birthday gifts are there on the island."

I had only listened to a portion of what she said, because I already knew that Rachel had written it all down for me. She knew that I was not good with verbal direction, especially when there were multiple steps in the instructions. It's like when I'm playing chess. I have a lot of trouble plotting out more than one move at a time, which makes me a horrible chess player. Mary can beat me easily these days, but I pretend to be losing on purpose. With Rachel, she just seemed to use too many words to explain her intent, and during the process, my mind would wander. She knew by now that I needed written instructions, but she would still attempt to provide them verbally as well. Despite my efforts to please her, I just don't have the same kind of brain she does. Call it ADD or whatever you want, but I've always had trouble paying attention to Rachel.

"I gotta go," Chuck blurted out as he grabbed his windbreaker to leave. I noticed that there were four packages of peanut butter crackers in the pocket. "I have to hit the pool."

Chuck swam two miles in the pool every day down at the YMCA. I used to tell him that aliens must look down on exercising humans and laugh. We swim laps or get on treadmills and walk in place for hours with only one purpose: to look better. And why would anyone take two hours of each day to swim back and forth a hundred times in some germ-infested public swimming pool. Even if that made you skinny, doesn't it make more sense to get on a bicycle and go somewhere? At least you saved the gasoline from having to take a car to the 7-Eleven to get your Slurpee.

"Thanks for stopping by, bro," I said, even though I hated using the word *bro*. It simply sounded awkward coming out of my mouth. It was like saying "dude" or "buddy." I was just not a dude- or buddy-saying kind of guy. People could probably be classified into distinct personality groups by those who use the word *dude* and those who don't. As Chuck walked out the door, I saw Dingo wagging her tail as if she needed to go out. I knew she was telling me to take advantage of this opportunity to go back to the green-door house. From our conversation about girls, Chuck had inspired me on where I would go next. I looked at my watch and I still had an hour before the birthday party.

"Come on, Dingo," I said as I reached for her leash.

"Don't forget the party! Three o'clock," Rachel called out from the next room.

"Got it. I won't forget," I responded as Dingo and I strolled out into the sunlight. That next hour would be one that would change my life.

Chapter 8

IF YOU CAN IMAGINE IT, IT IS POSSIBLE

As Dingo and I ambled down the street, I wondered if this green-door house was actually some kind of fifth dimension or time portal. A gateway to a part of heaven, perhaps? As many with near-death experiences have reported, when the door to heaven opens, we are welcomed in by our relatives and other departed loved ones. I have imagined that we are then invited to sit down and view a film of the "greatest hits" from our life. From accomplishments to other significant selfless acts, we get to review how we lived our lives. *Maybe that is what this house is all about?* I thought as I walked up the sidewalk toward the front door.

On this visit, Dingo and I went into the house without hesitation. She ran immediately over to the couch and I looked down the empty and dusty hallway. As I gazed ahead, I noticed there was a different door open this time further down the dark corridor. Dobie appeared again as he did before sitting on the brown couch with his legs crossed. He had a smile on his face as he motioned for me to come closer.

"I figured you would be back. Good to see you, Neil," he said pleasantly.

"I don't know why I'm doing this again. That first experience was literally a nightmare," I stated. "But I thought about it and I want to give it another shot."

"There is a reason for everything in this house," Dobie replied. "And I suppose you are back to return to one of your favorite experiences?"

"I am. How'd you know?"

"Seems logical once you figure out how it works. Let me guess, you want to go back to the big catch in high school? No wait, when you first adopted your kids?"

"Nope," I said, and suddenly I started to feel some nervous tension. "No, I want to go back to the first time I, you know, the first time."

"First time?"

"Yeah, you know, my first time," I said clumsily while trying to hide my embarrassment. "Her name was Cindy. Cindy Wintergreen. She was so pretty and everyone . . . well, my friends, they thought she was good-looking and . . . she was a year older than me and it was… it was her first time too, you know. So it was kind of a special night." I sat down on the chair across from Dobie and continued. "I was only seventeen and, well, I want to go back there and see her again. She was older and popular, and I really liked her, but I can't seem to remember what happened after that night, you know? I can't recall why it didn't work out with us. I want to experience that again . . . like you said, with the right frame of mind."

"And you don't see any problem with that?" Dobie said emphatically.

"No. Why would I?"

"Well, because you are married now, remember?" Dobie stated.

"Yeah. Sure, but I wasn't married then. And you told me that this is just me reliving it. It already happened. Why would it matter if I was married now or not?"

As I was saying this, I felt a tinge of guilt, but not as much as I should have. It had been over five months or so since the last time Rachel and I had been together sexually. While I hadn't technically cheated in our seventeen-year marriage, I occasionally felt it would be justified based on her recent lack of interest. After we adopted the kids, Rachel seemed to come up with almost any reason to avoid being intimate with me in the bedroom. Mostly, she would say that I needed to be way nicer to her to get her in the mood. And after months of complaining and feeling like an idiot for asking (a.k.a. begging), I just accepted the new reality. And when you get into your late forties, it just isn't that big a deal anymore. Rachel still looks great to me, but the days of physical thrills together seem to have past. So I thought going back to my first time with Cindy was the perfect compromise. It wasn't cheating. It was just remembering it again—in person.

"Okay," Dobie said, turning his face away from me. "If that's what you want to do."

"Wait. Why are you so against this? That night is part of my past, so it is a part of me. Like you said, maybe I can learn something from it that will help me. That will help my marriage today."

"I doubt that. But it is your choice, Neil. I won't stop you," Dobie retorted.

Dobie led me toward the open door in the hallway and I descended into the dark stairway. He followed right behind me.

"Are you coming too?" I asked.

"No. I'm just your guide, remember?" Dobie replied.

"Yeah, but . . . you won't be watching us, will you?" I asked shyly.

"I won't watch. Not this time. I'm just outside in case you need me for something. I wish you would reconsider, but you do what you have to do and we can talk after."

"Okay," I said as I stepped farther into the darkness. Once I hit the bottom stair, the dim light gradually revealed a slim young girl standing next to a large wooden bureau. It was Cindy, and there we were again, in her bedroom. I certainly felt like I was seventeen years old again in every respect. I felt vital and virile like I hadn't in many, many years. Cindy had just turned eighteen, but she was clearly very nervous as she fidgeted with her blouse. The room was mostly dark, but I could still comprehend how young and girlish she was. In many respects, she was just a child and, well, so was I. She was so pretty, and her body was just as I remembered it: very firm and beautiful. There she was looking at me seductively, and she seemed to want to do what we were about to do as much as I did. Why else would she invite me up to her bedroom? Why else would she dim the lights and put on a Dan Fogelberg album? The seventeen-year-old me was hesitating, but only because so many thoughts were entering my head at once.

As Cindy started to unbutton her blouse, I swiftly took off my T-shirt and threw my blue jeans on a nearby chair. Wow! I looked down at my stomach and it felt good to be thin again. I couldn't believe how much energy I had. It was as if I could jump over a building. Cindy inched closer to me, and I held her and kissed her passionately. She tasted so good and I could feel adrenaline rushing through every part of my body. As I continued to kiss her, Cindy reached down to touch me, and I nervously jumped backward a few steps.

"I'm sorry," I said. "I'm really sorry. I-I didn't expect that."

"Did I do something wrong? Do you not want to?" Cindy asked innocently enough.

"No, no. I mean, yes. I do. Definitely. It was my fault. I'm sorry," I said as I moved closer to her and removed her dainty pink bra. Cindy shyly moved out of the only light in the room as we continued to kiss. I was disappointed as I wanted to see her naked so badly. One thing for sure is that God made most men to be intensely attracted to the female form. It is an instinctive and powerful urge, and yet I wondered why it had changed for me and Rachel. When we were first married, Rachel and I made love regularly. I loved her body and we enjoyed being together. I remember how incredible I thought it was that I could now have a woman to make love to as often as we wanted and without any guilt. That was pretty much how it was until the years we were trying to have kids.

"It's time! We have to do it tonight," Rachel once remarked matter-of-factly while making dinner. My seventeen-year-old self would never believe that those words would not be a welcome invitation to intimate pleasure. But as I entered my late thirties, I still enjoyed sex, but it had become rote and even mechanical at times. While Rachel was still extremely attractive to me, it seemed we had done all there was to do as a couple in bed. She didn't want to experiment anymore, and the sex lost a bit of its luster. One time during our quest to become pregnant, I actually asked her if we could skip a night. I would never have believed this earlier in my life, but I just didn't feel like doing it. There was an Indians game on and for some reason that took priority. Pretty pathetic. And now we barely do it at all and only when Rachel wants to. We still get into bed together at the same time most nights, but it's only to read and then to sleep. We don't even cuddle anymore.

"What do you want me to do now?" Cindy asked while sensually rubbing my surprisingly hairless chest.

I looked closely at her face, and it was then that I realized just how young and innocent we were. What else would we do next? I guess when you have done this as many times as most adult couples have, we know what to do next. We know what to touch and what not to touch. We know what feels good and what doesn't. We know how to communicate with each other when we want to do something special or different. But when you're seventeen, and it's your first time, you don't know any of that. You only know you want to do something immediately! I was literally a bull in a china shop and poor Cindy was the delicate china.

But as we continued to kiss and fondle each other, I felt a huge sense of regret over what was about to happen. As Dobie had explained from the beginning, I knew that there was no stopping or changing my actions. And unlike a real time machine, I was just reliving the event and my actions were not going to be different. Cindy was a willing participant here, but I could not help but wonder why she was doing this. In fact, I wondered why would any girl her age be willing to do this? The guy is literally powerless over his urges, and it seemed to me that most girls knew that. I was enjoying the excitement of being with my first completely naked girl, but I wasn't enjoying the rest. And Cindy didn't seem to be enjoying this any more than I was. *What were we thinking?* I thought. The truth is, we were too young, and our minds were not ready for what this meant. I wanted to get out. I felt such a sense of shame.

So much for my memory of this being a really great time. It was not fun for either of us. And it led me to recall what did happen to us after this night. It was two weeks later before I even talked to her again and when I did, I was cold and distant. It wasn't that I didn't still like her. I did. She was pretty and popular. But I was only seventeen. I wasn't ready for a mature relationship, so I did nothing. It would not be the same between us and we couldn't pretend it didn't happen. Thus, I ignored her, and I am sure I hurt her feelings, but that is what we did in those teen years. I started to wonder if she still thought of me today. Wouldn't she naturally have some memory of this night? It was her first time too. She probably hates me, and I don't blame her. For a girl, the first time should be special and, well, this wasn't special in the way it was supposed to be.

As Cindy led me to the bed, my seventeen-year-old self followed. We kissed passionately as she kicked off her skirt and panties. Remarkably, I could feel tears welling up in the corner of my eyes. I didn't remember tearing up that night, but I did. I didn't remember being so nervous, but I was. And I know now why I didn't enjoy it that much. I was doing what most seventeen-year-old boys talked about doing. But teenage boys do a lot of talking and talking is very different than doing. As we progressed onto the bed, I knew what would happen next. We would have sex and she would wince from the pain. It must have been horrible for her and the bed sheets would eventually show signs of that being her first time. I wanted to stop it. What was I doing? How do I stop this? I couldn't. And I didn't.

Dobie was right. This was wrong in so many ways. And now I had to pay the price for it.

Chapter 9

BAD MEMORIES ARE LIKE CUTS THAT NEVER HEAL

I used to tell people that my primary goal in life was to be a good father. If I could do that, everything else would fall into place. After all, a good father is a role model to his kids. A good father is an adequate provider. He is honest and protects the family, fixes the cars, goes to church, etc., etc., etc. But as I aged, I realized that this supposition was not a goal as much as a requirement, a minimum standard of sorts. As the Bible states, even evil people love their own children.

When Dingo and I arrived back at our house fresh from reliving the Cindy Wintergreen experience, I saw both of my children sitting on the front steps of our home. Jessica was dressed in her green pants and Mary was reading a Harry Potter book. When I saw them, I immediately looked down at my watch, which read 4:15pm.

"Oh my gosh, girls. I'm so sorry."

Mary looked up from her book briefly and then continued to read. But Jessica just looked straight ahead at me without changing her expression.

"Look at that," I said, glancing down innocently at my watch again. "Wow, I totally lost track of the time. I must have, uh, well,... let's get going. Okay?"

"The party ends at five. We might as well stay home," Mary said emphatically. And then I saw a tear drop from Jessica's eye.

"Oh no. Come on. We can make it," I pleaded as I stepped around the girls to let Dingo into the house. "Let's go. I'll drive really fast."

"I don't wanna," Jessica whimpered as another tear trickled down her cheek. I felt horrible as I literally watched the hurt feelings developing in that little seven-year-old mind. These were the types of bad-parenting events that had happened to me as a child, times when my father said nothing or did things that hurt me to the core. I came home from middle school once with my report card and, for a change, it was mostly good grades and the comments were the best I had ever received. I couldn't wait to show it to my dad. I had really applied myself that year, and I wanted him to know it and be proud of me. I longed for a compliment from him, which I imagined would bring me all kinds of joy and pride. But when I got in the house, my father was sitting in his favorite chair reading the newspaper. Instead of going into the kitchen to grab a snack as I normally would, I went straight into the den. Not grabbing a snack immediately after school was an indication that this was really important news.

"Hey, Dad, check it out," I said as I handed him my report card. My father took the card and nonchalantly placed it on the lampstand next to him. He barely even acknowledged my presence.

"I'll look at it later. Go ... go do your homework or ... something," he stated as he continued to scan the opinion page in the newspaper.

"No, Dad. Look at it. Please!" I implored him. Waiting even ten minutes at this point for him to be finished with the paper would have seemed like an eternity. I wanted him to pay attention to me immediately. So I stood there refusing to move.

"Honey!" my father shouted out and up into the air above him.

"Leave your father alone, Neil," my mother called back from the kitchen. "Come bring the card in here. I want to see it."

I stared at my father for several long moments in disbelief as he continued to ignore my presence. The hurt and anger of that moment built up in me like the bubbles in a shaken soda can. I was about to pop. I was all of thirteen years old, and I felt like crying. Even a sensitive kid like me, though, knows that crying in front of your father would be the ultimate shame. So I grabbed the report card and turned and ran upstairs. I never did show him the card. He never asked, and I never mentioned it again. But that event stuck to me like it was tattooed on my chest—a really nasty tattoo, and one that I never wanted anyone, especially my Dad, to see.

"Mommy is going to be real mad at you, Dad," Mary stated as she nonchalantly flipped to another page in her book. I picked up Jessica and carried her into the house as tears continued to flow down her cheeks.

"Come on, honey," I implored to her. "Daddy made a mistake. We can still go for ice cream. You'd like that, wouldn't you? I will even let you get a double chocolate with sprinkles."

But despite my pleas and promises, Jessica only pushed and struggled to get me to put her down.

"I don't want any," she said as she finally freed herself of my grip and ran up the stairs. Clearly, Jessica refusing ice cream was a bad sign—a really bad sign. I turned around and Mary was now standing in the hallway rightfully staring me down.

"What?" I asked.

"Mommy said you needed to be home at three. We were waiting for over an hour," she stately matter-of-factly as she walked around me to go up the stairs.

"Hey, honey?" I said as Mary ascended the stairs. "Do we have to tell Mommy about this? Why don't you and me and Jessie go to a movie or something? Mommy doesn't need to know, does she?"

"Mommy will know, Daddy. Mommy always knows."

That was the absolute truth. Rachel had an uncanny way of knowing things it seemed she just couldn't know. It was some sort of ESP or something, and I never questioned her perception of anything. She just knew.

But what had happened to me during that experience with Cindy? How had it taken so long? Not only did I feel terrible about reliving the event, but now I had hurt my kids. I didn't mean to be so selfish, but the time had passed so quickly. I knew Rachel would go nuts when she found out about this and—what could I say? That I was back in time making love to an old girlfriend? Dobie was right. This was the wrong thing to have done. It was cheating or as close to it as you could get, and I was a willing participant. My body felt dirty and I wanted to shower off the shame of that memory as soon as I could. But I couldn't. I felt terrible and I had a feeling that things were only going to get worse.

Chapter 10

WE ARE ALL GOING TO BE WRONG ABOUT SOMETHING

I go to church most weekends, but I am still trying to figure out where I stand in terms of believing in Jesus, God, religion, and the purpose of this life. I see faith as something personal and very different than churchgoing. My father was a minister, so I was exposed to "church" and all the business of running a church from an early age. In one part of my mind, "church" was simply a bunch of people who have decided that "they" are the ones who have it all figured out. So they put their ideas and rules on paper and call it a religion. The fact that there are literally countless denominations and other faiths tells me that there are a lot of people who don't have it right but think they do. As I have matured, I am only sure of one thing regarding religion or belief systems in general and that is this: We are all going to be dead wrong about something.

When Rachel returned from her errands to find me and the girls sitting on the couch watching television, I knew that there would be no defending myself about missing the birthday party. Could I tell my wife that I was in a time machine and lost track of . . . the time? No, that was clearly not the plan to get out of trouble. I had decided that in this case, the best defense was no defense. I would simply admit I was wrong and take the punishment like a man. Or like the version of a man that I was trying to be in our marriage.

"Hey, gang, I'll have dinner ready in just a few minutes," Rachel said as she put her bags and keys on the counter. Normally, my job at this point was to take her car keys and put them on the key rack next to the garage door. Otherwise, we would all be looking for those keys for thirty minutes the next time she was ready to leave the house. Despite my wife's type A personality, her car keys were the one exception to her rule of putting everything back in its place. And when she would start looking for her keys, it was always a good idea to get out of her way or risk being trampled over and blamed as she ran through the house screaming out *"Who moved my damn keys?"* So I generally just subtly put them back on the key rack while she unloaded her things, but this was not the time to do that. Rachel stopped cold when she saw the wrapped presents still sitting on the kitchen counter.

"Oh, my god! How in the world did you forget the presents? They were right here. Didn't the girls remind you?"

My wife was so thoughtful that she not only got a present for the birthday girl, but for her sister too. I loved the generous side of Rachel. She was the friend who always brought food or cookies when someone was sick. She was the friend who would offer to get your mail when you were on vacation. She was the person who never forgot a birthday or anniversary. Once, my wife organized a book club party for a group of her friends. She spent the entire day working on the party food and other preparations and then, one by one, each friend called to offer an excuse for not making it. I was heartbroken for her, but she never blinked an eye or gave it a second thought. She just went on with her evening and the family enjoyed the appetizers she prepared. Her giving and kind spirit was not conditional or based on the expectation of getting something in return. In all my life, I have never known another person who was truly altruistic. But Rachel was.

I got up slowly from the couch, sauntered into the kitchen, and just came right out with it.

"I'm sorry, Rach," I said sheepishly. "I lost track of the time and we missed the birthday party."

"You what?!" Rachel screamed as she slammed her hand down on the counter. "How in God's name did you forget? I told you twice and even wrote it all down in a note for you. Are you an idiot or just trying to piss me off?"

Wow. That was way worse than I expected. This was clearly not the time for excuses.

"I messed up, Rach. I don't know how I forgot, but I forgot. I'm so sorry. When I realized the time, it was just too late."

Rachel went into the den to look at the girls who were paying enough attention to the television to allow her to let her anger loose in the kitchen.

"You are pathetic. You know that? I do everything around here and when I ask you to do one simple thing, you . . . you forget. I'm speechless. How could you forget?"

"I don't know. I'm sorry," I said in the sincerest tone I could muster. But there was a big part of me that wanted to react to her saying that she did everything around here. Didn't my making a living to support our family make even a small dent in that "everything" she was referring to? In the days when I was growing up, my father's only family responsibility was to work and provide an income. My mother did all the child-raising, household chores, etc. Even when I needed some fatherly recognition of my good report card, my mother took on that role herself. In our house, it was clear and settled. My dad had done his job simply by doing his job. He had gone to work, and it was my mother's role to do everything else and to keep us out of his hair. How had things changed so much in only thirty or so years?

"Do me a favor! Next time don't volunteer to do things that you have no intention of doing," Rachel uttered as she walked past me into the den. She then knelt on the floor next to the couch and looked at our children with the tender look that only a loving mother can give.

"Jessie. I'm so sorry that Daddy forgot the party. He just wasn't being a good father today. I will call Lisa's mom and explain, and we will have her over to the house this week, so you can give her your present."

"Okay, Mommy," Jessica said without even blinking an eye away from the television.

"Mary, I'm sorry for you too. I know you were going to play American Girl dolls with Lisa's sister. We'll ask her to come over too."

I watched from the kitchen as Rachel did her best to get the girls to understand. I felt bad, but from my vantage point, I was not getting a fair shake here. All I had done, as far as they knew, was let an hour of time slip my mind. Did that make me a bad father? For the most part, I was as much engaged in the life of our family as any father I knew. I washed dishes occasionally. I helped organize family trips or at least pay for them. I read to the girls most nights, unless there was a game on. I did other things too, but I always had trouble remembering what they were when arguing my point. So how could Rachel make me feel so bad about this one little incident? Gosh, compared to my father, I was a *Super Dad*. What was I doing wrong that made her think otherwise? Was this just the new generation of fatherhood? We do our jobs and are expected to do most of the mother's job too?

"Thanks for nothing," Rachel snipped as she passed me on her way upstairs.

"You're welcome," I quipped back before I could consider the wisdom of allowing sarcasm to enter our duel of words. While there are many things of which I know a little, I knew this one thing, this day, and it was crystal clear: I was in deep, deep trouble.

Chapter 11

GOOD MEMORIES ONLY GET BETTER WITH TIME

It was an away game and we were playing a rival school from a tougher side of town. We had the football back on our own twenty-five-yard line and we had ten yards to go for a first down. It was my senior year, and I was a two-way starter on a very bad football team. I played fullback on offense and linebacker on defense. At this point, we were winless with only a few games left, and this game looked to be another disappointing loss. Our quarterback was not throwing the ball well on this day, so we kept giving the ball to our two star running backs. It was my job was to block for them. I didn't mind. I was a good blocker and I loved to hit, so I didn't complain about not running the ball that much.

But on third down, the coach sent in an inside trap play where I would get the hand off. I was surprised they called it and even wondered if it was a mistake. I was not a third down back and I usually only ran the ball early in games before we were behind in the score. The trick to this play, though, as I had learned, was to delay a few short moments after the snap to give the left guard time to pull to his right and engage with the defensive lineman in the hole just right of center. On prior occasions, my energy and excitement had caused me to run right into the back of the pulling guard, but on this day, the delay worked, and the hole opened for me. I wasn't that fast, but I could be quick when I saw daylight, and I sprinted through the line and quickly into the defensive backfield.

It was a rare occasion for me to be this far downfield. I was a typical blocking fullback, and speed and fancy moves were not my thing. But on this play, I saw no one near me, so I turned on the limited speed I had and ran straight down the middle of the field. I must have been twenty or more yards downfield when I saw the defensive backs converging on me. I knew to put two hands on the ball as they would attempt to knock it loose, and I carried three of them on my back for another ten yards before I went down.

I didn't usually pay much attention to crowd noise, but I heard it this time and they were cheering for me. I was pulled after this play to get a chance to rest, and the coach congratulated me when I came to the sideline. What a great feeling that was. A true breakaway run, and I could hardly wait to get back into the game to run it again.

After a few plays, I did go back into the game and the play was called. But this time, the quarterback told me to switch places with the halfback and do the blocking of the tight end on the right side. When I asked why, he responded that he wanted someone faster to run the play. I went to the halfback position and watched as the faster back ran right into the back of the guard for no gain. The coaches and quarterback hadn't learned what I had learned, but they tried the play several times with the other backs instead of me. I even told them about the delay tactic, but they didn't listen. We lost the game, of course, but I still have a positive memory of my run and it still pops into my mind whenever I think of my senior season.

That game could be the time to go back to, I thought as I walked down the street. But for some reason, I feared that this memory would turn out to be different than I remembered too . . . or worse, ruined. I still wasn't sure what the purpose of this time travel house was for me, but I intended to find out. Did God want me to learn something from these events? Were there life lessons that I did not learn the first time they happened? Was He preparing me for something else? Was the easiness of my job a mistake in that I was not honoring the gifts God had given me? My best guess was that something was wrong with me that needed to be fixed. Why else would I need to go back and experience painful moments again?

"Listen," I said into the empty hallway while walking in the door. "I'm done with these . . . bad trips back. I mean, what's the point in that? I want to do a good remember when."

My brother and I used to call the recollection of our fondest memories "remember when" moments. This started when we would exchange our favorite stories on the long car rides to and from college. One of us would begin by stating "Remember when I . . ." or "Remember when we . . ." And then we would reminisce about something fun and most often about someone especially good-looking. Yes, we usually talked about girls, but sports successes were also thrown in from time to time like the football memory.

"This time I want to go back and relive one of the good times from my life. Okay? Let's make this one fun."

"Okay. We can do that," Dobie said cheerfully as he suddenly appeared next to me. I was so startled, I almost fell over. "How about we go back to one of your biggest successes? Can you think of one? I have one in mind."

"I was thinking football . . . but wait . . . how do you . . . what do you mean, you have one in mind?"

"I didn't mean anything by it," Dobie replied. "It's really up to you, Neil. Just tell me what event and I'll see if I can make it happen."

"Okay," I said, but I remained curious by what Dobie meant. "What event were you thinking of?"

"I know you liked that football run, but that is already a good memory. I was thinking of something that you might not have properly recognized was a bright spot in your life."

"Oh yeah, like what?" I asked incredulously. "So you can read my mind even when I'm not here in the house with you? What's up with that?"

"I know about you and I know your past. I was thinking of the class competition in college. You know the one . . ."

I did know "the one." There was this contest in grad school for the student who could come up with the most creative or inventive new business idea. Based on my love of cars, I created a computer-based car consulting service that was designed to help people know which kind of car they should buy based on their unique preferences and what they could afford. These car-buying services are commonplace today, but it truly was something new and unique back then. I worked with a professor on the database and completed the program in just under a month. There was nothing like it out there, and I won the class competition hands down. That was one of my proudest moments, and my parents came to see me get the award when I graduated.

"You mean the car-buying thing? Yeah, that was cool, but what could I learn from that? I won it. Case closed."

"Wouldn't you like to be there again? And experience that proud moment?"

"Sure," I said rather reluctantly as I knew Dobie had to have an angle for suggesting this.

"Well then, let's go. I believe we need to go through the last door on the left," he stated as he got up to lead me down the hallway.

We passed by the broken door handle and I went to grab Dobie by the arm to stop him, but my hand went right through him . . . like he was a ghost.

"Hey, stop. What's with you? I just went to touch you and . . ."

"Oh, sorry. I should have mentioned earlier, I'm not real like a human body. I'm only real spiritually," Dobie explained. "You are real and of this world. I am not of this world. Basically, I am only an illusion to you, but to me I am real. Like these experiences or trips to events that are going on here in this house."

"But you . . . I've seen you pet Dingo. If you are a ghost, then how can you do that?"

Dobie smiled.

"We have a special relationship with dogs. I can't really explain it, but they are kind of like one of us," Dobie said as we walked farther down the hall.

I stopped in my tracks directly next to the door handle that was broken off. I turned and looked closely into Dobie's eyes and tried to see if there was something different about him. His eyes were a deep dark brown, and his facial features implied a gentle disposition. Dobie was not unattractive, but he lacked any special characteristic to define his looks. He was average height, average weight, etc. In fact, if you described him, you might only be able to say that he looked just about like anyone else. As I thought about this, I wondered if that also described me.

"Let's go," he said as I stepped over the broken door handle.

Dobie motioned toward the last door in the hallway and I entered the stairway again, but this time I waited a bit on the top step to see if my eyes would adjust first so I could see better while descending the stairs. While standing there, I remembered I had brought a list of questions I meant to ask Dobie about the house and what this all meant. I went to reach into my pocket to get them when Dobie vanished, and then suddenly, there I was in the auditorium of my graduate school. At this juncture in my life, I was twenty-eight years old and still very much unsure of myself. As I listened to the professor introduce the topic for which we were gathered, my mind was full of worries about my future. My first job after undergraduate college was managing a restaurant. Then I worked at a hospital as an assistant administrator. In both jobs, the only thing I really liked about them was getting a paycheck. After six years of trying different things, I thought that graduate school would give me some extra time to figure out what I should be doing for a living or, as some call it, a career.

That word, *career*, for me, was elusive, as I wasn't cut out to be a doctor or a lawyer or anything that held a clear "career-type" definition. I just wanted to do something I enjoyed and get paid for it. After two years in business school, I had learned mostly that the top jobs in business were not for me. The executive ranks seemed like a huge meaningless game of chicken, and the guys with the biggest egos and the lowest morals held a huge advantage. Also, I was not a butt kisser and politicking for a promotion or recognition literally turned my stomach. So, despite having an MBA, I chose to work in sales rather than go into management. Sales to me was simply getting to know people and solving their problems. And you could do it without all those corporate nimrods looking over your shoulder.

The truth was, most of the top-level executives couldn't do what I did. Their game was too selfishly motivated to accomplish what good sales people do. In sales, we must win over our prospect and then keep their trust and confidence by helping them do their job. It's that simple, and for most of the past twenty years, I was at the top of sales earners in the company. I wasn't ashamed to work in sales, but I knew that this wasn't a point of pride for my father. Once after grad school, I was visiting my parents and my dad was out in the front yard watering the plants. I was heading out to take a jog and I heard my father bragging about Chuck to a neighborhood friend.

"My boy Ted (a.k.a. Chuck) runs his own finance business. Travels all over the world too. He is doing great and doesn't have to answer to anyone. Makes a lot of money, but I never ask him how much. I just know he is doing very well."

"What about your other son?" the neighbor inquired as I quietly moved closer to listen to my father's reply.

"That one? Oh, I don't know . . . he works in sales or something like that. He's not asking me for money anymore, so that's good," my dad said snickering. I cleared my throat loudly, so he would know that I had heard him.

"Oh. Hi Neil," my father said in surprise as I approached. "Didn't see you there."

I shook the neighbor's hand as my father pretended not to be embarrassed.

"Neil works for . . . what it is again, Neil? Some kind of paper company, right? I don't even know what he does, but at least he isn't living at home anymore. I got 'em both out the door and the Moreland Hotel is officially closed."

The neighbor laughed uncomfortably as I walked directly past my father. I made sure he saw my face. He knew I was hurt. But in truth, I wasn't as hurt as I normally would have been. I was good at my job and I knew my father didn't understand what I did for a living. He never asked me about it, but my father wasn't the inquisitive type. He knew I was doing okay financially and that was a huge relief for both of my parents. I often thought of writing a book about the modern world of sales. I had what I thought was a clever metaphor (or analogy) that described the business world as a set of integrated gears. They all need to move simultaneously and do their job to make the system work. But "sales" was the crank that turned all the gears. Without sales, the entire process would be stuck, just a non-moving set of gears (personnel, executives, and accountants with nothing to do except drink coffee and flirt with pretty secretaries).

"Attention, graduates and guests," the dean of the business school began, "if everyone will please take their seats, we can get started with today's program."

The dean's voice echoed into the room and slowly the chatter and clanging of chairs and feet died down and there was silence. Dean

Thompson was a handsome slender man who had once worked in the Reagan administration. He was an impressive figure who was lured to this little southern school by a big compensation contract. The school was trying to gain a reputation and having a figurehead leader was one way to attract better students. Funny enough, I had only seen him twice in two years and this was one of those times.

"We are going to start the afternoon by announcing the awards for the graduate business school program. As you know, we are preparing only the best of the best of the business world here and among those, we have a few that really stood out."

As the dean continued his speech, I looked around the auditorium for my parents. I was nervous and felt like I might throw up when the dean announced my name. I remembered that Chuck couldn't make it as he was traveling overseas, but my parents did come to the event and they even stayed one night in my not-so-elegant apartment. The other bedroom was open for guests as my roommate had left immediately after school ended and didn't care about going to the formal graduation ceremony. He had his degree and that was all that mattered to him. But to me, getting this award and my diploma meant a lot. Not only did I graduate with honors, I learned that I was a creative person and a good problem-solver. Most of my classmates spent their two years memorizing information in textbooks and I knew that just wasn't the real world. I applied my real-life experiences from work and found that I understood things better than most. Graduate school had proven to me that, despite my numerous insecurities, I was smart, and I did have something to offer the world.

"And the award for outstanding independent study for business school graduates is . . ."

My heart raced as it had before when this happened, and I feared for a moment that I might faint. "Oh God, please don't let me do that again," I prayed. But I didn't faint and the sound of my boring name echoing in the room actually sounded spectacular.

"Neil James Moreland."

As I rose to go get the award, which was a glass trophy about a foot tall, I looked out into the audience and in the direction of my parents. I smiled and immediately caught sight of my mother who was sitting on the left side of the room, about twelve rows back. But to my surprise, I didn't see my father. Where was he? Making a phone call? Wait a minute! This was different than I remembered it as I know he was there. As the applause concluded, I just stood there fixed at the podium.

"Thank you, Neil. You can go back now," the dean concluded.

I stepped slowly down from the podium and walked back to my seat with my head down so I wouldn't trip on something. But my mind was racing in confusion. I didn't remember the event like this. My father was there. I know he was. Someone was playing tricks on me. Was it Dobie? Was it God? I sat motionless in my seat as the dean gave out the other awards. I looked out again toward the audience and my mother smiled back. But all I could focus on was the empty seat next to her where my father should have been. Where was he? Had he not been there and I just blocked it out? If he came all this way to see me graduate, where was he when it mattered the most?

"Thank you, ladies and gentlemen, and let me conclude by saying one last thing to our graduates . . ." The dean paused dramatically before continuing. "Each one of you has a special purpose for which you were created. God put you on this earth to accomplish something incredible. Our job was to help you find that special something, but now it is up to you to make your mark. Leave a legacy that will be remembered. It could be something as great as finding a cure to cancer or as simple as inventing a new flavor of ice cream. But it all matters. Every contribution counts. But we also need to remember to give back something to the world. So go out there and find the purpose for which you were created. And when you do, remember to thank those that helped you get there. Think again of the persons who challenged you to do better and even thank those who put up obstacles. It was those people that molded and shaped you into the best version of yourself. Don't forget that, and may God bless you all."

The people in the auditorium stood and applauded. I had listened to what the dean said regarding thanking people, but all I could think of at that moment were the people who didn't support me. Or specifically, the person whose opinion mattered to me the most: my father.

As I went to leave the stage, I accidentally kicked over a thermos. It was my thermos and I remembered now that I had filled it with alcohol. I was so nervous about getting this award and walking to the podium that I thought I might need a drink to calm me down. I picked up the thermos and carried it offstage with me as we filed out of the auditorium. I also remembered what my father had said to me when they were getting in the car to leave the next day.

"Who carries a thermos with him to his graduation ceremony? I mean, who does that?"

My mother, always the compassionate excuse-maker, told me not to worry about it.

"Your father has been under a lot of stress lately, dear," she said while attempting to hug me goodbye.

That was it. That was what happened that day, but it was very different than my memory. Over the years, I had somehow blocked out the fact that my father was embarrassed when he saw me carrying the thermos. I had blocked out the fact that he wasn't there in the auditorium when I got the award. Later in life, I talked to a therapist who told me that I needed to forgive my father for everything he had done or not done. She suggested I write him a letter to explain how I felt, and then destroy it without giving it to him. In the process, I would symbolically be moving on and getting over the hurt feelings. In all my years, I don't think I ever got any worse advice. By not confronting my father on any of these things, I had allowed the hurt feelings to fester. I had allowed him to have a persistent negative power and influence over me. And the proof of that was that I never did go on and do anything special. My award still sits in my office today on a dusty shelf next to a box of tissues. I once knocked it over and chipped a piece of glass off the bottom corner. It seemed appropriate to me that the trophy was broken. I was broken too.

Chapter 12

OUR PERSONALITY IS MOSTLY DEFINED BY THE THINGS WE FEAR

I tried to shake off the impact of another emotionally draining trip back in time, and now nothing in my present life seemed to be going right either. My wife was mad at me and I had another (literally) growing issue. I was in such bad shape physically that even my fat jeans weren't fitting me anymore. I had tried all kinds of diets over the years and they all worked. Like the guy that quits smoking over and over, I could lose weight any time I wanted, but I just couldn't keep it off. I used to be able to sweat off the pounds with exercise, but the gym held no allure for me anymore either. At one time, I loved playing competitive team sports, but I was getting too old for all that now and so were my friends. Even one of my favorite sports, tennis, had become a strain on my aging body. That left simply dieting and eating healthy food as a way to stay slim. No thanks.

The real problem, I thought that morning as I watched my urine hit the water in the toilet bowl below, was that I had nothing to look forward to. My life had progressed from a series of "wait until next week" to "next year" events and was venturing toward "when I retire" thinking. That type of thinking was clearly not healthy, but so many of us live our lives with the idea that when we retire, we will finally do all the things we always wanted to do. Then most of us retire and we get sick right away and die. Or worse, we get dementia and can't remember where we live or the names of our children. I do pray that no matter how God intends for me to go, I do not want to die without a memory of my life. But, for now, I was stuck in a funk about my job as it just wasn't providing any type of satisfaction anymore. This led me to think that at age 50, I was still not sure what I wanted to do for a living. How pathetic is that?!

In college, my brother and I used to talk about what we would do if we had a million dollars. That, of course, was in the day when having a million dollars meant you never had to work. So, let's change that to 10 million dollars and adjust it another 10 percent annually for inflation. The truth is, I had no idea what I would do if I won the lottery or ever had that kind of money. I did know for sure that if I had been a rock star in my twenties, I would likely be dead today. The lure of drugs and women would have easily won over my weak constitution. I had heard once that you should think hard about what you would do if you instantly came into a ton of money and *that*, they say, is what you should do for your career. In other words, if you were rich and had no money worries, what would you do? Would you go to France and paint? Enter acting school? Apply to be a cartoon character at Disneyworld? What? As fun as this imagination game seemed, it still seemed to me that making money had to be a part of any career decision, right?

One of the career advice books I read encouraged you to think of what you "would" do if you had no fear of failure. In other words, just think of what you would want to do if there were no negative consequences. Despite the attraction of doing whatever I wanted for a living, that also seemed a bit crazy to me. I've seen a lot of people who fearlessly chased their dreams and still ended up a failure. The odds of making it big in music or in Hollywood seems like they are 10 trillion to one. Even getting rich in the business world was highly unlikely unless you got incredibly lucky with an invention or hit a rise in the stock market perfectly. Most of us did jobs that paid just enough to get by, and that was true of almost everyone I knew.

My wife and I were on our first big vacation together in Paris one summer and there was this guy displaying his artwork on the street near the Louvre. This long-haired, dark-skinned beatnik-looking guy had painted several renderings of the city. The paintings displayed were, in my opinion, very well done, and when I asked him how much, he replied in a southern US drawl, "How much you got?" How sad is that? Here was this talented American painter in Paris, living out his dream, and yet he was willing to sell me his precious art for not much more than the cost of the canvas and paint. From the looks of him, I presumed he lived on the street. I gave him the meager amount I had in cash at that time and he took it. I felt so badly for him that I promised to come back the next day and buy another painting. I didn't actually do that, but that moment was somewhat of a dream-breaker for me. Whoever was writing all this "go for your dreams" crap needed to take some time to read a book on budgeting.

It is a fact. No matter how cool it would be to go after a dream job, the job still must cover the bills. Water, food, clothing, heat, etc. are not options. Just ask anyone living on the street today. They will tell you. Money matters and the more you have, the better. It's only those super-rich spoiled brats that let money destroy them. You know the stories. We watch them on tabloid shows. But these people are the rare case or exception to the rule. We love to hear the latest idiot move from a wealthy pampered celebrity, but there are hundreds of good rich kids who will tell you what we all basically know at heart: MONEY ROCKS!

As I struggled to get dressed that morning, I could tell that the girls and my wife had already left the house. I normally didn't sleep through all the histrionics of getting the girls ready for school, but on this day, I did. Since I was raised with boys, I had no idea how difficult it was to get a girl dressed and ready to go out. From choosing the right blouse to go with the skirt to matching the shoes, hair ribbon, etc.—it was entirely too complicated and intimidating for me. As a guy, I simply wore whatever shirt or clothing article that was clean and still fit me. (And like my younger daughter, any garment at the bottom of the dresser drawer simply never got worn.) I picked my shoes based on where I was going that day and if the pants were dirty, I simply wore them anyway. It wasn't that hard. No one would ever say "That Neil Moreland sure can dress," but they also don't realize that I save literally thousands of hours per year on "primping" that I can use to do other more productive things, like watch television.

I clicked on the television in my bedroom as I tried to match two loose socks together. The morning news anchor was interviewing a doctor who was talking about ways to maintain a healthy colon. They had drawn diagrams on the screen indicating the size of the colon and where food tended to get trapped. It was disgusting. It dawned on me then that, unlike Superman, we were probably lucky not to have X-ray vision. I don't think many of us really want to see underneath the shirts or the skin of another person. For the most part, people are far more attractive in clothes. Have you ever seen pictures of people at a nudist colony? They basically ruin the idea of being naked by being naked all the time. My experience with Cindy in the time machine had also proved to me too that we should only be naked with people that truly love us. In my experience, only alcohol seems to diminish that rule.

I would normally click off the news hastily, but the next segment of the program promised to reveal the secret to a happy and fulfilled life. I needed to know that secret! I needed something to lift my spirits. I was dubious, however, because if they knew the so-called "secret," would they really be willing to share it for free on the news? Wouldn't you at least want to get a book deal out of the thing? No, I think most people are happy or unhappy and there isn't a lot you can do to change that. And today was not a happy day for me. In fact, I felt almost . . . depressed. It wasn't just feeling sad mentally; I was physically depressed. For the third straight time, my time-machine experience had left me feeling worse about my life. Even the event I believed to be one of my greatest memories turned out to be a sad day with my father's absence during the awards. Thus, I vowed that day to never go back to the house and mention the experience to anyone. It sounded crazy enough to me. For some reason, I guess I needed to relive those moments and recognize that life was—I don't know—hard.

After brushing my teeth, I threw on my Tony the Tiger baseball cap and went downstairs to walk the dog. I loved that cap. My girls got it for me on my last birthday since they knew I really liked Frosted Flakes. It only cost twelve bucks, but you also had to send in like a hundred box tops along with a check to get it. They were even asking me to eat the cereal up faster, so they could get more box tops. Fortunately, I could eat frosted or sugary cereal every day for breakfast if Rachel would buy it. But she doesn't, so I am left to buy a box at the local mini-mart each time I stop for gas.

I went down the steps from the bedroom and felt eerily curious as Dingo would normally be rushing up to greet me. But for some reason, there was no sign of her. When I entered the kitchen and saw the table empty and the counters clean, I knew something was wrong. I looked in the garage and Rachel's car was gone. I called again for the dog and heard nothing. I entered the hallway and then I saw it. There was a small envelope sitting on the hall table. It was addressed with only *Neil* written in pencil on the front and I knew what it meant before I picked it up. Rachel had left me.

Chapter 13

"WHATEVER" IS THE WORST WORD IN THE ENGLISH LANGUAGE

Over the last few years, I had slowly and gradually lost contact with my father. It wasn't a purposeful alienation and I wouldn't call us estranged from each other. We just talked less and less, and then ... we didn't talk at all. As a result, my mother and I talked less too. I loved my mother and she tried her best to get us to visit them, but there was never a need for us to come up with excuses to avoid going. We always had them: school projects, sickness, business conflict, etc. To make a six-hour trip (by car) or to put four people on an airplane, you also had to plan far in advance. And I wasn't itching or willing to plan a trip to Louisville, so we simply didn't go there. Rachel's parents lived just five miles away, so I had basically adopted them as my immediate family. We had lots of involvement with them and since Rachel had four siblings, we were always busy with them too.

As I looked at the note on the table, it was as if I realized at that precise moment that without Rachel, I was in big trouble. My family, my identity, and all that I had was suddenly gone or in pieces. I knew instantly that the remainder of my meager life would mean nothing if I was alone. Even my kids, although they would always be my kids by law, suddenly did not seem as much my kids anymore. She even took the dog. Until that moment, I had not realized how much of "me" was wrapped up in "her." Did I have to let things get this bad and risk so much to realize that I needed my wife?

What an idiot! I thought as I picked up the little white envelope. I opened it slowly and read:

Dear Neil,

I can't take it anymore. I need a break from you.

I took the kids to my parents and I'm going to need some time apart.

The girls needed the dog with us and I'm sorry about that. I know you will miss her.

Please don't call me. I will call you when I'm ready.

Get some rest and enjoy the time to yourself. I know that is what you want anyway.

Rachel

Every word of that little note was like hearing fingernails on a blackboard. I couldn't bear to read it again or to even hold it. I immediately dropped it in the trash and went to get in my car to go to her parent's house. I had to see her. I had to see the kids. I couldn't let this happen. I started the car and pulled out into the street without thinking of what I would say or do once I got there. But as I drove, I realized I was instead heading straight for it. There it was just staring directly at me. The green-door house. Maybe that was what this time travel craziness was all about. "That's it!" I surmised. "That's why I've been doing these trips back in time. The time machine will fix this." And with that, I pulled into the driveway of the old house and stormed in through the green door.

"Where are you!?" I screamed. "I need to see you. I need to see you now!"

As I started to walk down the hallway, Dobie appeared suddenly and startled me so badly that I almost collapsed.

"Geezus!" I said as I regained my balance.

"What's wrong? Did she leave you?" Dobie asked somberly.

"You know she did," I stated while shaking off the jitters from being snuck up on again. "That's what all of this is about, isn't it? You knew it would come to this and you . . . you are going to help me fix this. We are going to go back in time and make things right again."

"You can't do that," Dobie responded. "I told you. We can't change the past. We can only—"

"I know what you said. I . . . I don't want . . . I want . . ." I uttered struggling to find the words. "I want you to take me back. Take me back to when I first met her. I need to be there again. Maybe I can figure out something that can help me make things better. Can you do that at least?"

"Follow me," Dobie said as he led me toward another open door in the hallway. When I descended the steps, I was trying to remember when I first met Rachel. Was it at a party? A bar? How could I have forgotten something so important? I vaguely remembered that Chuck's wife had introduced us, but I couldn't remember exactly where or how we met. Down the steps I went, expecting to meet up soon with Rachel's pretty face, but that didn't happen. When I got to the bottom stair, I was staring instead into the face of . . . my father.

My dad was only twenty-seven years old when I was born. This youthful face was one I only knew from pictures. But there he was, a young man again. And he was holding me. I looked up at him and all I could feel was a complete sense of comfort and safety. This man, I thought, would protect me. He would never drop me or hurt me. He will take care of me. The feeling of love that I felt was so incredible that I believe I actually did relieve myself into . . . my diaper. That's right. I was a baby. I tried to talk to him, but only spit came out of my mouth.

"Did you have a good day, Neil? What did you do?" my father asked as he swung me gently from side to side. I tried to talk again, but again only slobber.

"Daddy is going to buy you and Teddy a new swing set. Did you know that? I'm going to set it up outside the house this weekend. And I will push you on it as much as you want."

As I carefully examined my father's face, I saw a more peaceful man. But more importantly, I saw his love for me. This was all happening before the bad report cards, the arguments, and the lectures about school and how I was screwing up my life. Before the time I came home drunk and passed out on the kitchen floor, before I lost my car and my wallet, etc.. One of the things I always hated to hear my father say to me was the word *whatever*, and he said it a lot. For example, if I related something to him about my day, no matter how important or how trivial, my father would seem as if he hadn't heard me and would mumble "whatever" in response. I have tried, but I can't find a way to use the word *whatever* in a positive way. It is an awful word. As a result, I hate hearing it to this day.

"Daddy loves you," my father said as he gently put me back down into my crib. He stood there looking adoringly at me, and I smiled back at him. I wished I could talk so badly. I wanted to ask him why he had stopped loving me. Was I that bad a kid? Sure, I drank and got wild with my friends now and then, but wasn't that just like most teenagers? I was fairly popular. I did okay in school. I wasn't a drug addict or a convicted felon. Not yet anyway. Why couldn't he love me for who I was?

As my father turned to leave, I started to cry as I really wanted him to come back. "Waaah!" I emanated, which meant "Come back, please!" But he didn't. Even worse, he turned off the light and closed the door. I was scared of the darkness, so I cried even harder. I cried so hard that my eyes hurt. My body hurt. I felt pain all over and I screamed again and again for help. Wouldn't anyone come to ease the pain? Didn't he hear me? Why wasn't he coming back to comfort me? I cried louder and louder and then suddenly I was back on the couch facing Dobie.

"Come on! What the heck was that about?" I asked. "Can't you even once give me one thing I ask for?"

"I'm sorry, Neil. I don't make the decisions. I'm just your guide. Remember?" he responded.

"I don't get it. I ask you to take me back to when I first met Rachel. And you make me into a stinking baby?"

"That baby is part of who you are, Neil. All of your life is part of you. The entire time you live on earth is linear, but your life is not. Your life is a collection of events and it is circular. The experiences make up who you are, and you are the events. That is what this house is all about."

"All I just heard there was blah, blah, blah," I blurted out. "I need you to explain it clearly. I need to understand how being a baby is supposed to help me."

I got up and paced the room as I tried to think of what to do next. Remembering the experience, I reached down to feel if my pants were dry or not. They were dry. Thank God. Then I remembered about my notes and the list of questions I had about the house. I reached into my pocket, but these were the wrong pants. I tried to remember all the things I wanted to know about this house, but all I could think of was Rachel.

"I need to get Rachel back," I said somberly.

"I know, Neil. I want to help you. I really do," Dobie replied.

"I asked you to take me back to when I met her and you . . . how is me being a baby going to get Rachel back?"

"It has something to do with it, I think. It has to," Dobie stated.

"Can you ... can you try again? Let me go back so I can learn what I need to do to get her back? Hey, I know, let's try that door with the broken handle. What's down there? Do you know?"

"I only know that it is not open for a reason, Neil. I was told to be very careful with that one."

"So what? Let's do it. I want to go down there. How much worse can things get? Right? Let's go."

"Not so fast, Neil. I'm not sure you are ready. I was told explicitly to be very cautious about that door. It could really screw up your future if you aren't careful. I don't even think I am allowed to let you at this point."

"Hey, wait a minute," I said as if I had discovered the answer to a very difficult crossword clue. "You aren't even the person in charge of all this, are you? Tell me! Who gives you these instructions. Who decides where I go? "

"The guy in charge told me," Dobie retorted and in response I somehow resisted the urge to punch him in the face. Instead, I took a deep breath and tried a different approach.

"Okay, how about this? What is the name of the person who ... who told you ... the guy in charge? Is it Jesus? Buddha? Batman? Who?" I asked, confident now that this would get me the answer I desired.

"Oh, that is easy," Dobie said. "His name is Cloyde."

"Claude?" I attempted to repeat, not sure I had heard him correctly.

"No. It's KaKa ... LeLe ... Oid," Dobie responded.

"His name is Cloyde. The guy in charge is named Cloyde? What kind of name is that?" I questioned. "It sounds made up."

"Cloyde is from a different time. It actually will become a very popular name sometime in the future. You'll see."

"I doubt that, but anyway, what is it that this Cloyde does?" I asked.

"Cloyde oversees all the guides and he gets to decide who goes when and who goes where and who helps who. You see?"

"Is he your boss? Is he like an angel?"

This was starting to resemble the movie *It's a Wonderful Life*, which just happens to be one of my favorite movies.

"All I know is that there are limits and Cloyde advised me to avoid that door until . . . or unless . . ."

"Unless what?"

"Unless you were . . . desperate," Dobie concluded.

"Desperate? Look at me. My wife just left me. I'm fat as a pig. I'm totally sick of my job. I would say that I am desperate at this juncture. Wouldn't you?"

"Not really. Actually, I have seen some desperate people and . . ."

"I want to go through the damn door . . . damn it! If you need to get Cloyde down here, then do it!" I demanded, hoping to end this discussion and get on with it.

With that, Dobie got up and led me over to the door with the broken handle. He picked up the broken piece and placed it carefully back onto the stem where it belonged. He jiggled it back and forth and the door did not budge. I reached out to help him, but Dobie put his hand up to indicate that I needed to step back.

"You're just a friggin' ghost," I said. "Let me try it."

"I got it," he said as the door opened, and a gust of moist air billowed out like the mist from a dense jungle. There was a howling that sounded like a dog that had just been hit by a car. The odor was very unpleasant, and Dobie and I instinctively backed away.

"Uh, maybe, I . . . I don't know about this," I said while trying not to inhale the awful smell emanating from the staircase.

"I agree. How about we try this some other day?" Dobie remarked as I retreated a few more steps back.

"Yep. Let's do this one . . . later," I said as the door closed by itself.

Dobie gradually disappeared, and as I turned to leave, I noticed that the small envelope from Rachel was sitting on the floor in front of me. *How the heck did that get here?* I thought I had thrown it out, or . . . had I? I wondered if I had dropped it. But when I picked it up, the note inside was gone. Instead, there was just a picture of Rachel and me from early in our marriage. She looked so beautiful that I could hardly stand to look at it. How had I let this girl get away? I concluded that I must be one of the biggest idiots on the planet. And at this point, almost everyone I knew would agree with that statement.

Chapter 14

DREAMS ARE EXPERIENCES AS REAL AS LIFE ITSELF

Ever since I was a child, my dreams have always been relatively vivid. I used to keep a notepad next to my bed, so I could write down any good thoughts that entered my head during the night. It has led to some great story ideas and sometimes even a decent song would come out of it. The dream I had this night, however, was not my normal type of dream. It was more like the feeling I had when I was back in time. In some ways, it felt more real than even my real life did. In this dream, I was an actor in a movie and I was playing the role of the captain of a large passenger ship. The ship was a large modern cruiser with all the amenities we expect on luxury liners today. I was at the helm and alone on the bridge when I saw what appeared to be another large cruise ship heading directly toward me.

I turned the captain's wheel to the right (hard starboard?) and braced for what appeared to be an inevitable impact. But the impact never happened, and we passed right through the other ship like it was a cloud. My heart beat profoundly as I looked out over the officer's deck and saw what appeared to be several people moving about below. When the cloud diminished, I could see the gray ghostly figures of dozens of people wandering around on the deck. And then I realized that these were the people that had been on the other ship. Their faces were ashen and withered and they had bodies, but no feet. They floated around on the deck like they were dancing with each other and some of them floated up and appeared in the window in front of me. They were the faces of many of the people I had known over the course of my life. Teachers, friends, classmates . . . and they kept coming. More and more of these ghosts. Each time a new face appeared, the name of the person would pop into my head and I would remember how I knew them. They say that when you die, your life flashes before your eyes. Was that what was happening here?

I woke up and was very relieved that I had only been dreaming. I wanted to tell someone immediately about the dream, but with Rachel gone, I had no idea who to call. Chuck was not an option as he would only use my request to talk as an excuse to go out and drink beer. I love my brother, but he was only good at being there to help you ignore your problems. So my mother was literally my last resort. And she would listen to me talk about Rachel, which I desperately needed. I dialed the phone hastily and waited for a response, hoping it would be my mother and not my father.

"Hello," my mother answered in a shaky tone.

"Hey, Mom, it's Neil. Sorry it took me so long to call you back."

"Oh hello, dear. How are you?"

"I'm not so good, Mom," I said, preparing to tell her everything I could about the dream and my current situation.

"I'm sorry, Neil, but I just can't do this right now. I'm so sorry."

"Do what?" I asked, feeling suddenly hurt and that something must be seriously wrong.

"You haven't called in months and now . . ."

There was a surprising silence on the other end of the phone and I knew immediately that my mother was crying.

"What's wrong, Mom? What happened?" I said, forgetting my troubles for the moment.

"There's nothing you can do. So don't worry about it."

"What?! What is it?" I said indignantly.

"It's your father. He's . . . well, I don't know how to put this really. It's such a strange thing."

"What is it, Mom? You're freaking me out."

"He's just not there anymore," my mother said between sniffles.

"What do you mean he's not there? What does there mean?" I asked.

"His mind. He's gone. He doesn't even recognize me half the time," my mother uttered barely above a whisper.

"What happened? What? How?" I mumbled. I just couldn't process her statements. How could he be gone?

"It started a few years ago, but you didn't notice. And then when he was really losing it, you were nowhere around. We just dealt with it on our own. You didn't need to know or be bothered."

"Bothered? Mom. He's my father. You're my mother. I know he and I have issues, but he's still my father."

"He can hardly dress himself anymore. It's like . . . it's like living with a child."

As my mother said these words, the image I had seen of my father holding me flashed back in my head. Is that why I had relived that event from my life? Was God trying to tell me that something was wrong with my father?

"He's in a good place now," my mother said with her voice returning to normal.

"Wait. What do you mean? Where did he go?"

"He's in an elderly care facility where they specialize in his condition. I just couldn't cope with it anymore. I tried. I really did all I could. But I am just really, really tired."

"So. This is like . . . Alzheimer's?" I asked, hoping I had pronounced the name of the disease correctly.

"They're not calling it that exactly. It's dementia," she said before blowing her nose. "He's had a lot of mini-strokes. But the last one was a doozy."

My mother had been using that word *doozy* as long as I could remember. I was shocked to learn later in life that she had not made up the word. Apparently, it was a description of a very large automobile called a Duesenberg. When people saw the mammoth vehicle passing by, they would say, "There goes a doozy!" I liked thinking my mother made up the word better.

"So . . . he's not living at home anymore?"

"No, dear. He's not. It's been some time now," she said.

"Well, can we visit him at the, um, in the elderly house place?"

"You can if you want. It's not a pleasant sight, Neil. He has lost so much weight. They practically must force-feed him now. It's like he wants to die. Maybe he does. I don't know."

"Mom, I can't believe you didn't tell me any of this. Does Chuck know?"

"Ted knows he's sick. But I have trouble explaining things to him. He never seems to be paying attention when I talk to him."

"Mom, he doesn't pay attention to anyone," I said, hoping to ease the pain caused by her self-centered oldest son.

"I convinced Ted to come home this weekend. You should come too. If you can."

"Of course!" I said emphatically. "I'll call Chuck and we will ride together. We will be there."

"Good. I'm glad. You can stay with me at the house. It feels so empty here now. It will be good to have someone to keep me company. Wait. A minute ago, you said something was wrong, dear. What is it?"

"Oh, it's . . . nothing, Mom. I'm fine," I said, hoping that would soon be true.

"Are you sure?" she asked.

"I'm sure. I'll see you Friday."

"Okay, dear. Goodbye."

"See ya, Mom."

I hung up the phone and sat down on one of the living-room chairs. *My poor mother,* I thought. She deserved better than for her life to end up like this. She put up with my father for all those years and now she would have to play nursemaid to him as his mind slowly wasted away. It made me realize, though, how important marriage is, especially at the end. Who else besides a devoted spouse would want to take on the duties of nursing an old man or woman in their final days? Helping them shower, dress and, yes, even changing their adult diapers. But there was my mother, ever faithful to my dad and taking care of him. I know it killed her to put him into an assisted living facility, but she wouldn't have done it if it wasn't the best thing for him. It would likely drain their entire savings for him to live there, but my mother wouldn't have it any other way. I had to wonder if anyone would do that for me. And at the present time, the answer to that was clearly no.

Chapter 15

A SYNONYM FOR ANY FAMILY IS "DYSFUNCTIONAL"

My brother Chuck drives a Porsche 911, which has only two seats and hardly any room for luggage. I drive a four-door family-sized sedan, so this pretty much tells you who the cooler brother is in my family. Nevertheless, there I sat in the cramped passenger seat of Chuck's sporty coupe with two bags and a briefcase on my lap for a six-hour drive. I had offered to drive, but Chuck wanted to show off his new sports-ride to his buddies at home. I had to pay for the gas, of course. Now that he was divorced, Chuck wanted to put the word out on the street that he was back on the open market. I figure a Porsche helps you do that. Given that Chuck was fifty-one years old, I'm guessing he was trying to impress the daughters of his old high school friends. Sad but true.

"Let's go out on the town when we get to Louisville. I want to try out some new clubs near the campus," Chuck announced as he adjusted his fashionable Ray-Ban sunglasses.

"I'm not goin' to any fraternity bars with you," I said. "Let's just spend some time with Mom and support her. I'm sure she's lonely. And she sounded so tired on the phone."

"You are such a mama's boy. You know that?"

"Yeah, I know," I said in retreat, but he was right. I had always favored my mother. I appreciated that she tried her best to make up for the lack of support from my father over the years. Sometimes I think I took out more of my teenage anger on my mother than my father because she actually cared enough about me for it to matter. If I got mad or gave my dad the silent treatment, I don't think he would even have noticed. A therapist once told me that all families are dysfunctional, and she is probably right. But my mom would sometimes know without asking if I was down about something. She would even come into my room at night and just sit there as I told her about some problem or issue. I used to say that she had a free ride to heaven when she died as she was such a good person. The only mystery to me was why she married such a curmudgeon. And yet she supported him in every manner. Hearing her frustration with his illness or disease on the phone was unusual for her. Clearly, this disease thing or whatever it was had taken a toll on her.

"Sounds like Dad is really out of it," Chuck said as he sped along at eighty-five miles an hour.

"Yeah. Mom said he barely even recognizes her anymore," I responded. "When did you last talk to Dad?"

"I'm not sure, really. After my divorce, I guess. He was pretty cool about it," Chuck said.

"Dad was cool with it. Your divorce. You're kidding?"

I was truly shocked that my father would be cool about any non-conventional event in the family that could tarnish our Ozzie-and-Harriet reputation. My father once told us that we were an extension of him and that when we messed up, it made him look bad and he wouldn't have it. When I came back home from college, my father gave me a set of rules to live by if I wanted to live in the same city. Those rules included (1) no public intoxication, (2) I had to come to church every Sunday I was in town, (3) I had to volunteer for something at the church, and (4) I couldn't embarrass him no matter what I did, said, or thought.

"Dad even paid for my legal bills?" Chuck continued. "Hey! You know why divorce is so expensive?"

I shook my head no.

"'Cause it's worth it," Chuck emoted before emitting a prodigious laugh. I ignored the joke since I had already heard it at least fifty times since his divorce.

"No way he paid for it," I exclaimed as I knew my father would see this a failure on Chuck's part.

"I didn't have any money back then. Debbie really took me to the cleaners," Chuck explained. "But I was going to pay him back. I promised him that, but"—Chuck started to laugh—"guess I won't have to now."

"Good one, Chuck," I said in disgust.

"Oh, come on. Dad is old. This shit happens. Heck, it is in the genes. His father went senile and so will you and me. Most likely you, for sure."

"Why me, for sure?" I asked incredulously.

"'Cause you are the brainy one. Like Dad. Really smart people get this stuff first. It's a historical fact."

"Do you even know what a historical fact is?"

"Yes," Chuck said confidently. "A historical fact is that you are going to get senile. It's genetic engineering."

"How in the world did you ever graduate from college?" I asked in true amazement.

"I sat next to really smart people," Chuck remarked unashamedly. It was true, after all. Chuck had 20/10 vision and was one of the best copiers in the history of the University of Louisville. Plus, that infantile fraternity house had copies of almost every test ever given at that school.

"So you want to go see Dad right away or go to Mom's house?" I asked.

"Let's go home and, uh, we can take Mom out for dinner first. You treat."

"Why me?" I asked curiously.

"You have all the money, that's why."

"You make way more than me, cheap ass," I responded back.

"I don't get to keep it and, besides, do you know what college is going to cost me for those ingrates? I'm going to have to work until I'm ninety to pay off those tuition bills," Chuck added.

One thing almost everyone in our circles knows is that Chuck is tight with the dollars. Don't get me wrong, he likes to spend money; he just likes to spend it on himself. When it comes to sharing the tab or check, Chuck's wallet goes as dry as the Sahara Desert.

"I'll pay for dinner. But I may be needing to watch my cash too. I won't have Dad around to pay for my divorce."

"Say what!?" Chuck exclaimed. "You and Rach going splitsville?"

"Yeah. Well, maybe. She left me on, uh, earlier this week," I said somberly. "Took the dang dog too."

"No shit. Get out!" Chuck remarked in disbelief. "I'm shocked. I thought you and Rachel were good. Man, I guess it can happen to anyone. What happened? She catch you playing around? Some chick from your old job? Wait, that therapy girl. The one working on your neck. You shacked up with her, didn't you, you sly dog?"

"No. Not me, Chuck. I'm not like you."

"Ooh. That was cold, bro," Chuck replied. "I'm not the scum you think I am. I only started cheating after Debbie did. She went out with that fucking muscle-head from her gym first. I knew something was going on there. Shit. Fucked me up, big time. I had to get some tail on the side too or I would have gone nuts. I'm still not over it. Shit, man. As that song says, love hurts. Who was it that sang that song? Narnia?"

"It was Nazareth," I said, fairly confident that they were the group that sang it. I knew for sure it wasn't the fictional place in the C. S. Lewis chronicles.

Still, I was mystified as this was the first time ever in my life that Chuck revealed any level of human emotion to me or maybe ... anyone. I was so surprised that I could hardly speak. Like my father, Chuck kept his feelings to himself and I was not sure what to say here. He kept driving and facing forward, but I could see some dampening in the corner of his eyes. I didn't want to push for anything more, but I had to find the perfect comment to distract him. I knew this was humiliating to Chuck and that he instantly regretted letting me in on his pain.

"How about those fucking Browns? Can you believe they got even worse this year?"

As the words left my mouth, I knew how stupid they sounded. Chuck was not a football fan and never cared much for the Browns. He only followed college sports and mostly ice hockey. Chuck would probably have been a great ice hockey player, but he broke his leg when he was in ninth grade and it didn't heal properly. To this day, Chuck walks with a slight limp, but it's hardly noticeable unless he's in a hurry. But the broken leg was another chapter in Chuck's life that we never discussed. I knew it set him back and killed off his athletic dreams. But with Chuck, you just knew not to go certain places. And I didn't.

"Fucking Browns suck. They should just forfeit all their games. Who needs them?" he responded.

"The city of Cleveland needs them. We don't have much of anything else to do in northeast Ohio," I said laughing, in hopes that it would help break the tension.

When we pulled into my parent's driveway, the house looked remarkably older than the last time I saw it. The black seal-coated driveway was now a light gray, and the surface cracks from years ago had turned into deep grooves. The hedges were overgrown and the paint on the eaves was dried out and crumbling. As we got out of the car, I tried to remember the last time I had visited. It was probably four or five years ago, but the change since then in the house was dramatic. Like my parents, the house had gotten old too. One thing I have learned about houses is that they always need work and attention. When a house is not cared for properly for even a few months, it starts to take on a look of neglect. It is almost like the house becomes depressed and simply let's itself go. Kind of like me.

"Hello boys!" my mother said as she strolled out of the front door.

"Hey there woman," I said as Chuck got out and kissed her on the cheek.

"Looking good for an old lady," Chuck said playfully.

"I'm trying, but the wrinkles are catching up with me. There's no stopping them now," my mother stated as she hugged me tightly.

"Wrinkles aren't nothing, Mom. Least you have all your hair." I smirked.

"I saw an old lady at the pool the other day with blue hair." Chuck chuckled. "And half of her head was nothing but dried-out old skin. She was in the lane next to me. I was probably sucking in all that flaked-off old skin as I swam."

No one laughed at this disgusting image while I helped grab Chuck's luggage from the small trunk. He left mine sitting on the seat, of course.

"I don't care about my hair anymore," my mother remarked. "Just let it go gray. Seems to fit me better than the red shade I had for all those years."

"It looks good, Mom. I like it better," I said, not really remembering a time when my mother had red hair.

I am actually a big believer in letting your hair and skin age gracefully. In my opinion, the actresses and actors who have had plastic surgery look worse. Rachel would say that we only notice the bad surgeries, but I don't think so. As soon as people start messing with their faces, they never look right again. And I'm sure with most of them it started innocently enough. They do one Botox injection, and someone says they look nice. So they do another, and no one says anything. So they keep doing them hoping for another compliment until someone says "What the fuck did you do to your face?" And then it is too late.

"Are you boys ready for dinner? I made pot roast," my mother stated proudly as she opened the door to let us in the house.

"Pot roast?" Chuck said with a smirk on his face as if he had just swallowed some sour milk.

"What actually is pot roast?" I asked. The truth is, I really didn't know. Was it a hunk of a cow? The stomach? Whatever it was, I didn't see the sense in putting part of a cow in a pot and cooking it. Even I could see that this couldn't be healthy. My mother ignored my question and simply headed inside as we followed.

"I thought we were goin' out to eat," Chuck said before my mother could explain.

"I want to stay in. I've been living on restaurant food for months. I want to cook for someone again. I hope you don't mind."

"Nope. I could use some home cooking," I said as we crossed over the threshold and into the living room. "But do we have to eat a boiled cow?"

When we set our bags down on the floor, the first thing I noticed was an odd smell. It was a smell I had known before, but I just couldn't place it. It was sort of like mothballs, but that wasn't exactly it. I picked up my bag and walked down the hallway toward the bedrooms and noticed that the normally tidy pictures on the wall were now crooked and very dusty. As I turned into the guest room, it hit me. The smell was the same one I had acclimated to when I worked at the cancer hospital the summer after sophomore year of college. The hospital specialized in hospice care for those with no hope left. It was, for lack of a better term, the smell of death.

Chapter 16

THE SURPRISE IS ALWAYS IN THE LAST PIECE OF CAKE

As a child, I used to think my father was the tallest person on earth. Even though he was only six feet four inches, I used to tell my friends that he worked as a clown in the circus. Back in the '30s and '40s, he was abnormally tall, and I had fun telling my childhood buddies that fabrication. By today's standards, he is still tall, but not a circus freak. I did not inherit my dad's tall genes. In fact, I turned out to be a very average five foot ten and one-half inches tall. I think this is the exact average height of men today, but that average may include midgets, dwarfs and/or little people. I don't know the proper term anymore, but I seem to be shorter than most everyone I know, so I doubt my height is average.

When we arrived at the rest home and went into his room, I saw my father sitting on the edge of his bed. I thought at first that he was watching television, but when we entered, it was clear that he was just staring ahead at . . . nothing. There wasn't even a picture on the wall and yet there he was staring ahead like he was watching the six o'clock news on a big news night. For my father, whenever he was watching the news, it was an important news night. "Shhh," he would say to us. "Can't you see what is happening in the world? This is serious!" It is, in fact, the job of the news station to make the news appear to be important, but how could every night contain something earth-shattering? The fact that there was an outbreak of tensions in Somalia was not big news. It was and has been a problem for decades. But to my dad, hearing about this was far more important than the score of my game or the results of my chemistry test.

"He's having a good day," my mother whispered as we filed into the little room with one twin bed, two chairs, and a small dresser. "They told me he ate his entire breakfast. He hasn't been eating much these past few weeks, so he must have sensed you two were coming for a visit."

My mother set her purse down on the bed and walked in front of my father's blank gaze to get his attention. He looked up slowly, but there was not a spark or even a faint glimmer of recognition in his eyes. Normally, when he saw my mother, he would smile and perk up no matter what. My father looked over at me and then at Chuck and then back at my mother.

"Who are they?" he asked, looking at Chuck with a twinge of angst. Chuck's eyes darted back to my mother in surprise, but for some reason, I was prepared for him not to know me.

"Those are your boys, dear. That's Theodore, our oldest, and that one is Neil. They are our boys," my mother repeated.

"Harrumph" was the sound that emanated from my father as my mother motioned for us to sit in the two chairs near the end of the bed.

"They drove here all the way from Cleveland just to see you," my mother stated proudly.

"Harrumph," my father said again.

"Hey, Dad," Chuck said in a cheerfully fake manner. "This place ain't so bad. I saw some decent-looking nurses downstairs. I already claimed the brunette. Okay, Pops?"

"I'm locked in here like a rat," my father retorted.

"They keep you confined for your safety, dear," my mother responded. You can leave anytime you want as long as there's someone with you. You know that, don't you, dear?"

"Harrumph," my father grunted again as my mother opened the drapes and moved a vase of nearly dead flowers into the light.

"Hey! I've got an idea. Why don't the four of us go out to lunch? The entire family, just like we used to," my mother announced cheerfully.

"What family?" my father growled. "My family is gone. Moved away. They moved to Texas twelve years ago. Livin' on a ranch outside Waco or something."

I looked at Chuck as if we had just heard a piece of nonsense, and then it hit me. My father was talking about his family. It was his mother and father who had moved to Texas, but that was back when he was in college. It was not twelve years ago; it was over sixty years ago.

"I'm not hungry and they make me eat," my father complained as he pushed himself back onto the bed.

"The boys came all this way," my mother said politely while rubbing my father's arm. "Let's just go downstairs to eat. And then you can come back and . . . and . . . we can play cards or watch something on television. Okay?"

"I don't want to," my father said curtly. "I don't know you and I don't know these two . . . people. Now if you don't mind, I want to go back to bed."

My mother looked at me with eyes pleading for me to say anything. But my mind was blank. I looked at Chuck and he shrugged his shoulders and then my father said something that surprised us all.

"Wait. I know you," he said, looking directly at me. "Aren't you the kid that ate that entire cake?"

What the heck? Was he referring to my birthday party? I was turning eight years old and my mother made a chocolate sheet cake and had hidden a Kennedy half-dollar in one part of the cake. The idea was that some very lucky person at the party would eventually find the coin in their piece of cake. A great birthday party game, but ... but back then, I just had to have that coin. I was eight, for Pete's sake! It was my birthday and so before any one of my five friends came into the dining room, I started cutting into the cake to try to find the coin. It wasn't in the first six pieces, but I kept taking bites and cutting more of the sheet cake. Wouldn't you know it; the silver dollar was in the last piece of cake that I tried. The mess was incredible and there was chocolate cake all over the table, the floor, and me. When my father walked in the room, he took one look at me and yelled for my mother. My mother rushed into the room thinking that someone had just swallowed a bottle of pills.

"What?! What happened? Is anyone hurt?" she asked in a panic.

"Look at your dumb kid," my father stated to my mother and in front of the assemblage of family and guests outside the kitchen. "He ate every piece of cake before we even came to dinner. What a goof!"

"What were you thinking, honey?" my mother pleaded while wiping my face with a napkin. "You are going to be sick."

"I was just ... I wanted the silver dollar," I said as innocently as I could. "It's my birthday."

"Oh dear. Well, it is your birthday, I guess. But did you have to eat the entire cake?"

"It was in the last piece," I explained.

"Okay then, you get to keep it," she said, smiling politely while motioning to the others to sit at the table.

"No, I don't want it now. Dad ruined it."

My mother pushed as much of the cake back into the original position as she could, which meant that she still intended to serve the cake even though it now looked more like pudding.

"Your father loves chocolate sheet cake. I wish you could have left him a decent piece," she said as she went to empty the crumbs into the trash.

Here we were. Forty-three years later, and that is what my father remembers about me. He can't remember my brother's name (which is the same as his), but he can remember one of my childish screw-ups. This dementia thing is one wacky disease. I have often worried what the deal is with Alzheimer's and heaven. Does our brain go up there before we do? How can our memories be lost? They are part of us, right? Doesn't the soul have a memory? If not, what is left of us when we die? The events and memories are who we are, and the green-door house was proof of that. It seemed perfectly clear now. There was no escaping or forgetting the past no matter how hard I tried.

Chapter 17

IF IT REMINDS YOU OF EDDIE HASKELL, DON'T DO IT!

The next day, my mother was up early in her kitchen cooking Spam. Yes, that's right. Spam! The so-called meat product that came in a small blue can and smelled like a combination of pig's tongue and cow shit. The only thing possibly worse for you was something called Vienna sausage, and coincidentally it also came in a can. Someone once told me that it was made from the gook inside the hoof of a horse. I doubt that's true, but it did look like it. I had not smelled Spam in seventeen years as Rachel always got nauseous at even the sight of the stuff.

"How can people eat something like this?" Rachel would say. "There cannot possibly be anything more gross. I'd rather eat a piece of turd."

Rachel loved using the word *turd,* and I always thought she looked cute saying it. She was such a petite girl and when she said crude things like this, it made her look even girl-ier. In fact, in all our years, I had never heard Rachel pass gas or leave a bad smell in the bathroom. How is this possible when scientists tell us that the average person passes gas fourteen or fifteen times a day? Nevertheless, as far as I could tell, she never did do anything like that. And with Rachel, I knew if she did and I heard it, she would die from embarrassment. And I would have had a field day teasing her, so I'm sure she went to great lengths to avoid the possibility of it ever happening. She has never even allowed a small one to sneak out in front of me. Remarkable.

As I dressed for breakfast in the little guest room, I saw a framed photo of my father and four other men on the nightstand. I had a rule in my house that we would only put up pictures of the people we knew outside the family. We didn't need to see pictures of ourselves. It just seemed vain to do that. Why do you need to see pictures of people you see all the time? Pictures on display should be objects or places we want to remember. That was what got a framed place of honor in our home, and Rachel completely agreed with that philosophy. But my parents' house was different. There must be a hundred pictures of the two of them. All of them posed hugging each other or holding hands. My father even had a painting commissioned of himself and my mother. While it seemed a bit obnoxious to me, it didn't to my parents and they displayed it with pride in the entrance hall to their home.

In the picture on the nightstand, my father was evidently on a fishing trip with who I assumed to be some fellow ministers. My dad is holding up a small fish. His peers are pointing at him and smiling, so it must have been a joke of some sort. Maybe fish are supposed to be a lot bigger than the one he was holding. I don't know, but it was obviously a staged picture to commemorate the event. The sad thing about it was that I had never gone fishing with my father . . . or camping . . . or even to a movie. I'm not sure he ever went fishing again besides this one trip, but he sure looked like he was having fun. My father did not drink, so it wasn't an alcohol-related good time. This was just him being the leader of a pack of ministers. My dad was awfully good at leading people, and everyone I knew thought highly of him. So, despite our many differences, I was proud that my father was so well-respected.

I was able to get a real inside look at how my dad operated one summer when I asked if I could work at the church to make some extra cash for college the next year. My dad agreed but warned me that

I had to be on my very best behavior. And that I was not to expect any special treatment from him. What else was I to expect, given his strict nature? But on the surface, I was excited to be spending time with him where he worked and thought this might have some positive impact on our relationship. As the summer progressed, however, I started to wonder if he even worked there. His office door was always closed, and I hardly ever saw his car in the lot. As I got to know my way around the place, I realized that most of my father's activities during the week were not done in the church at all. This was a big church congregation (over a thousand people), and the church owned property, schools, and other businesses around this part of Louisville. He only worked from the church office on Mondays (for staff meetings) and on Sundays, of course, for services.

Since it was summer, my job at the church consisted mostly of doing outdoor stuff like picking weeds, mowing the grass, and generally cleaning up the grounds. Different things came up on a day-to-day basis and I did them. It was a good job for a college kid and I enjoyed working outside. One time when I did see my dad, he simply walked right past me as I pruned some bushes in the front garden. I waved to him and he nodded back as if to say, "Get back to work, you weirdo." The pay on this job was below average, but I had to admit, I was enjoying the work. That was the case anyway, until my father had an idea.

"What we need here . . ." my father announced to the maintenance supervisor who was within my earshot, ". . . is a patch of ivy in front of the church sign. Something pleasant and, uh, green. I'm thinking pachysandra and then plant some—I don't know—daffodils or something like that too."

I'm pretty sure my father couldn't distinguish a daffodil from a daisy, but that was all he needed to say, and the entire grounds and maintenance crews sprang into action.

"I'll get the flowers from the nursery," the head groundskeeper said to me. "Neil, this is going to be your baby. We can transplant the ivy from the back of the church. I'll have some guys bring it up to you in wheelbarrows. You can start planting the stuff right away."

The church sign was an impressive stone structure in the front of the church facing the main road (a six-lane thoroughfare). To this day, I like to drive by the church when I am in town to see the place where I spent those next few weeks on my knees planting (not praying). As the church workers scrambled to their respective duties, I walked outside and surveyed the job site. As I did, I realized that I would be very visible to the passing cars and thus every cute girl who lived in the city. My friends would see me there too. So I began wearing sporty T-shirts with cut-off sleeves to look as cool as possible.

The job was as simple as this: Take a vine of pachysandra. Dig a hole six inches deep. Fill the cavity with the end of the vine that has the roots. Bury it and water generously when the day was done. Repeat approximately ten ka-jillion times. Not much to challenge the mental energies, but at least I didn't have to ask for help or instructions. I just started the job and tried to make visible progress each day. I was a few weeks into the planting when I got some surprise visitors.

"Hey, Neil," my high school buddy Rich shouted out from his car. He played on the football team with me in high school, but he was a year younger. "Take a break and come have a drink with us."

I looked up at the clock on the church steeple and it read 2:30.

"I can't, guys. Gotta work until four thirty. I can meet you after."

"Come on," Rich said. "Who's gonna know? Your old man runs the place, right? You can do whatever you want."

I suddenly got a vision of Eddie Haskell of *Leave It to Beaver*. And if you watched that show, you would know those types of invitations from Eddie never turned out well.

I stood up and looked over at the car to see my other friend, Mason, drinking a beer. He had one of those foam cozies on it, but I knew it was beer. He also just had that look of a guy drinking a beer. It was a hot summer day and I had made a lot of progress on the planting. My father, as usual, was not there, and I hadn't seen my supervisor in over an hour.

"I guess I could, but ..."

"Come on, Neil. Get in. You got a change of shirt there?" Mason said as he looked at my very cool but dirt-stained shirt.

"Oh shit, that's right," I said, looking down at what was now pretty much a filthy brown rag. "I can't go anywhere like this. You guys go. Have fun."

I felt a sense of relief as I knew immediately that this was the right decision. And not having a clean shirt gave me the excuse I needed to remain good with my friends and stay where I was supposed to be—at my job.

"Hang on. We'll come over to you. I got some news," Rich said as he put the car into gear and drove slowly ahead. The guys then pulled into the adjacent driveway and parked in a no-parking zone and got out. I got up and brushed some of the dirt off my pants and noticed that Mason was bringing his beer with him. I looked closer and saw that Rich was also carrying a brown sack which had something heavy in it.

"Guess the shit what, Neil?" Rich said as he approached me.

"You have a venereal disease," I responded.

"Get this," Rich stated proudly while ignoring my comment. "I got a late acceptance letter and got into fucking MIT. Can you believe it? M-I—fucking—T."

As the words were leaving his lips, Rich pulled a glass bottle of tequila out of the bag. It was one of those half-pint-size bottles that you always saw in the movies. The type of bottle you could put back into your coat pocket after taking a swig. I believe that these small bottles in a bag are an often-used movie metaphor to indicate that the person drinking is in a bad state. Or is that an analogy?

"Get that out of here," I demanded immediately.

"Come on, man. You can do a shot with me, right?"

I smiled nervously as Mason took a long swig from his beer.

"No. Shit no. This is a church, you moron."

"What the fuck? Come on," Rich implored as he unscrewed the cap. "You can't take one fucking shot? I'm celebrating!"

Mason put one foot up on the wall of the garden in front of the stone sign and Rich took a sip of his tequila and then handed the bottle to me. While holding it, I imagined then that every car that drove by the church was either my father or a cop. But my dad was not in his car right then. He was standing right behind me and with his big right hand he swooped down and knocked the bottle out of my hand. Mason instinctively turned and ran toward the car while Rich scrambled to pick up the unbroken tequila bottle. My father moved in my direction and I seriously thought he was going to punch me in the face. In fact, he probably would have if the traffic had been a little lighter that day.

"Get out. All of you! Get out of here," my father screamed as his face turned a bright red.

I knelt down to help Rich find the bottle cap, and my father kicked my hand away. When Rich saw that, he immediately turned and ran toward the car to join Mason.

"I wasn't drinking, Dad. They just stopped by and—"

"Get out now before I do something we will both regret!"

I had seen that look a few times before and I knew he was capable of doing something we would both regret if I did not get out right away. He had that type of temper that made you think he could actually kill you—and not even regret going to jail for it. I saw him lose it once with Chuck after Chuck dented his new car. Chuck was a senior in high school and had not asked permission to use my father's car to go to a football tailgate party. Some drunken idiot at the party probably ran into it while Chuck was carousing and getting liquored up. Chuck claimed he didn't know how it happened, but there it was—a healthy unnatural impression on the right fender. When my father saw it, he took Chuck by the throat and lifted him off the ground with two hands. I have never seen Chuck so scared, and when my father let him go, we both knew he was lucky to be alive. Therefore, I knew better than to mess with my father over this. So I dropped my garden trowel and began walking slowly toward the front doors to the church.

"Not that way," my father shouted. "You walk around the back, so no one sees you. You look like . . . shit."

That was the first and only time I ever heard my dad curse. It was a shock and I knew what it meant.

"And don't bother coming home tonight. You are not welcome in my house," he said.

That is what it meant.

Chapter 18

THE WORLD IS A VERY LONELY PLACE WHEN YOU LOSE YOUR BEST FRIEND

We don't say it to each other, but I love my brother Chuck. Our brotherly bond was strong, and we simply knew that we would always be there for each other no matter what. It is almost remarkable that we were raised in the same household as we were different in so many ways. He handled his divorce without even once asking for me to listen to him vent about it. He didn't want or need to talk about it or at least didn't appear to. He just swallowed the pain and went on with his life. Unlike Chuck, I was only a few days removed from getting Rachel's note, and I was already a complete mess. I needed to talk to someone badly. But Chuck being Chuck, I knew I would need to look elsewhere for a shoulder to cry on. And with my mother handling all she could with my father, I couldn't go to her. As a result, I didn't know where to turn.

Life on this planet is very lonely when you don't have anyone to talk to about your problems. Throughout most of our marriage, I could talk to Rachel about anything. She was a great listener. A part of me wanted to call her to talk about "us" and how much I was hurting, but my instincts wisely told me that it was still too soon. I could ruin any chance for reconciliation if I jumped the gun. She needed this time to be alone, and if I pushed her in any way, it would be the end of us for sure. She needed me to be strong and to let her do what she had to do to get our relationship in better perspective.

"Are you still coming with me?" my mother said from the hallway outside the guestroom.

"Oh, uh, sure," I said, not knowing what she meant or where.

"Chuck is going to go see some old friends, so it will be just you and me today."

"You and me to do what?" I asked.

"To visit Dad."

Oh boy. I didn't know that I had agreed to another visit with my father. The first visit was painful enough, and I had no desire to go see him again.

"I'll get my purse," my mother said as I tried to think of something to get out of this. Unfortunately, I had no excuse, and I did want to do something nice for my mom. She too needed someone to talk to now, especially with my father in his current state. So I got my jacket and we hopped into her ten-year-old Buick LeSabre. I volunteered to drive, but my mother shook her head as she climbed into the driver's seat. The problem with my mother driving, however, was that she pulled the front bench seat so close to the steering wheel that I had to practically sit sideways to fit my legs under the dash.

"He was so happy to see you yesterday," my mother said while pulling out into the street without even a glance to see if another car was approaching.

"You think so? He seemed pretty out of it," I commented while pulling my seatbelt as tight as it would go.

"I think he knows more than we think he does. His brain just can't process it the way it used to."

"How long—I mean, when did he start getting like this?"

"I saw some signs, I don't know, four or five years ago. He would forget complete conversations that we had just had. Then he started missing appointments and not paying the bills. I had to drive everywhere with him or he would get lost."

"You're kidding?" I said in true wonder. "I had no idea."

"I finally got him to go to the doctor and they did some tests and found he had a substantial loss of cerebral function . . . in the frontal lobe."

"Wow!" I exclaimed. "And the frontal lobe is . . . ?"

"It is the part of the brain that has to do with memory and reason. His judgment was simply gone or very poor at best. It was during that time, that he . . ."

My mother hesitated in mid-sentence and I knew something bad had happened.

"What? What did he do?"

"Your father sent a check to the Episcopal Relief Fund."

"Wow," I said again. "Wait. That's okay, isn't it? You like that place?"

"It was more money than we had in our entire account. He just wrote it wrong. I had to ask them to send the money back. Imagine the embarrassment. Our checking account was overdrawn for the first time in our married life."

"Wow!" I exclaimed again while my mother drove twenty-five miles an hour in a forty-mile-an-hour zone. The traffic behind us was probably backed up for ten miles.

"I knew it then. I had to do something. He didn't want to go into the home, but I couldn't handle him on my own anymore. If he left the house, I had no idea if he would come back. And one day, he . . ."

My mother began to get tears in her eyes. She tried desperately to hold them back, but she couldn't.

"What, Mom?"

My mother pulled the car over to the side of the road and parked. She took a long deep breath before continuing.

"He was gone for over six hours. I thought I had lost him for good. I thought he might even be dead. But they eventually called."

"They?"

"The police. He finally stopped at a gas station to ask where our street was. He was ten miles from home and a nervous wreck."

"Wow" was all I could seem to say to any of this.

"So I knew I had to do something. Insurance covers some of the medical cost, but these places are so expensive and then there are the drugs. If it's experimental, Medicare won't cover it. I don't know what to do sometimes. It's like this disease . . . this mind thing, it is going to ruin us. I don't get it. He is such a good man, but it seems like God is ignoring him, and after all the years he served Him in that church, I just don't understand it."

My mother buried her face in her hands to cry and I put my arm around her shoulders.

"I'm so sorry, Mom. I'll do whatever I can to help. I promise."

"I know you will, dear. I knew I could count on you."

I'm not sure my mother truly believed I would help that much, but it was nice to hear her say it.

"So, is he getting worse?" I asked.

"It's a progressive disease, son. They can slow it down, they think, but I haven't seen signs of that. Every week seems to be a new low for him . . . and for me."

"Man," I said deliberately, realizing that I had said the word *wow* too many times already. "I guess it's for the best . . . him being in the . . . memory place."

"Yes. I suppose. I feel so guilty sometimes. But I just couldn't handle it," my mother confessed. "I visit him every day. He never likes it when I leave, so I don't tell him I'm leaving anymore. I just tell him that I'm going to the bathroom and then I don't go back. He doesn't realize the difference anymore."

As my mother said these words, another set of tears ran down her cheek. I had only seen my mother cry like this once before, and it was at her mother's funeral. My mother and her mother did not get along very well, and they were not speaking when my grandmother passed away. Her mom was from money, and status and position were very, very important to her. My grandmother would almost always wear a fur coat out of the house no matter what the weather. She drove Lincolns and Cadillacs and my mother grew up to rebel against that type of showy pretention. I think that is one of the reasons my mother married my father. He had something other than money that mattered to him. I presume it was a calling from God of some sort because being a minister is no easy job. Instead of one boss, you have hundreds (the congregation), and they all think they own a piece of you. My father never complained about it, but my mother told me once that he hated the committee meetings at church. The more money a parishioner had and often the more they gave, the more they wanted to get their way. Yet my father held on strong to his decisions in those meetings. He commanded respect and got it. That was never the case for me.

"You know," my mother began as she wiped her cheek. "He really does like you."

"Who? Dad? Yeah, right!"

"He does. He's just shy and uncomfortable with you. You two are different, but he admires you."

"Get out, Mom. The man always hated me."

"Oh goodness, dear. He doesn't hate you. He loves you. You boys are everything to him."

"Okay. Sure. Right, Mom."

"I'm serious. He talks about you all the time. Or he used to."

"Oh yeah? If that is true, then why didn't he bother to be in the room for my awards ceremony ... when I got that award?"

"What? Neil! What are you talking about?"

"The graduation awards ceremony. He wasn't even in the room when they called my name."

"Yes, he was. Of course, he was," my mother remarked with determination.

"No, he wasn't. It was just you. I looked out in the ... the audience and it was just you. Dad's place was just an empty seat."

"And that's how you remember it? Well, you are wrong!" my mother stated defensively.

"No, I'm not, Mom. I remember it exactly. I was just there. I just relived it."

"You ... what? What do you mean?" my mother said, looking over at me curiously. I scrambled to come up with a way to explain it without going into the entire time-machine concept.

"I mean, it is like ... it's like it just happened. I can't get it out of my mind. Why wasn't he there? Why would he leave the ceremony right at that time? Did he have to go make a phone call? What could be more important to him than seeing me get an award? It's like he didn't want to see me succeed. Maybe that's why he couldn't stand to sit there and watch it."

"Goodness me, Neil. He was there. I remember it well too. He went up front to get a better picture of you accepting the award."

"What?!" I blurted out subconsciously.

Suddenly, my mind was racing in confusion. Had I spent all this time thinking the wrong thing about that event? Why else would the time machine take me back to that moment in time? I was sure it was to witness his absence and to remind me that he never cared that much about me.

"Those pictures of you on stage. The good color one with the diploma and that award. The one we had framed for you. Dad took it. He even picked out the frame. How else do you think we got those pictures?"

"I figured the school took them. But . . . but I didn't see you after. I never . . ."

"That was your choice, dear. You told us that you had plans with your friends, so we left right after the ceremony. But he would have stayed. He was proud of the award . . . and of you."

This could not be happening. Suddenly I was feeling a rush of guilt over having such evil thoughts of my father. Yet it was consistent for me that he would have missed this event. He had been absent so many times in my life when I needed him. Football games, baseball games. He was never there when I caught the ball or made a long run. But even if he had seen it, he would never have said anything about it. I wanted him to acknowledge me and he never did, so I assumed he didn't care. Plus, he and I were not close, and I blamed him for that. After one of our typical arguments, he once told me that he loved me because I was his son, but he didn't like me very much. Funny, but I think that is the way God thinks about me too. But was there something else going on here? Something subconscious in my mind? Had I recreated this event in my mind to fuel my bitterness and keep it going? But why did the time machine take me back to that moment and show me the empty chair? How could Dobie have gotten this so wrong?

"I'm ... I'm ... in shock," I said wearily to my mother.

"You think too much sometimes, you know that?" my mother replied.

Truer words had never been spoken.

Chapter 19

BEING DIFFERENT DOESN'T MAKE YOU WRONG

There were many times in my life when I felt that my father and I were on completely opposite wavelengths. He gave us the impression that he never did anything wrong as a child and for all we knew, that could have been true. Yet, unlike my dad, I was a curious and inquisitive kid and that can often get a young child into trouble. One Christmas, for example, my mother gave my father a small hatchet to help him cut branches and limbs down from overgrown trees. My father liked a well-kept yard, and he often spent whatever free time he had working on the trees, hedges, grass, and gardens. But as soon as I saw that tree cutting tool, I knew I had to try it out. The hatchet came in a nice leather casing and he left it leaning next to the fireplace when he returned to the church for the Christmas Day services.

As soon as we knew for sure he was gone, Chuck and I took the small axe outside with us to see how well it worked. Chuck was eight at the time and I was seven, so we had a good sense that even touching the axe was a huge violation of my father's rules about using his tools. He would go berserk whenever he went down to his shop and found a screwdriver, hammer, or wrench missing. As a result, we were absolutely forbidden to touch any of his tools without asking first and even then, he usually said no. Nevertheless, the new hatchet was simply too big a temptation to resist.

The question for us at that time was what to do with it. We started by trying to chop into one of the maple trees in the front yard, but the hard wood was simply too strong to yield to our efforts, so we tried some of the tall pine trees. With those, we were able to quickly penetrate the soft bark, but we couldn't cut much more into the tree than the external layer. After trying a few other trees in the yard with the same negative result (other than injuring them badly), we decided to take the hatchet into the backyard and take a whack at some of the smaller fruit trees that were located on the side of the garage. Our yard at that time contained a wide variety of trees bearing fruit such as oranges, tangerines, figs, grapes, and even bananas. One at a time, we chopped down each of them completely as their soft fibrous composition was easier to penetrate with the new and very sharp axe.

My mother was in the kitchen doing the dishes when she looked out the window and saw the top of one of the banana trees swaying back and forth. Knowing there wasn't much wind, she knew instinctively that something was wrong. What she couldn't see was that beneath the canopy were two young Paul Bunyons taking alternating swings at the base of the tree. My mother rushed out to survey the damage, but it was too late. Chuck and I had completely choppeed through the entire array of fruit trees. When we saw my mother rushing toward us, we knew instantly that the trees were probably able to bear much better fruit if they remained planted in the soil.

When my father learned of the offense, he spanked both of us with a paddle, but he knew the instigator of the crime was me. But at seven years old, I couldn't understand why he was so mad at me. He was always out in the yard cutting down things and I just wanted to be like him. It seems like a funny story to tell now, but my father didn't see any humor in it. It is just another bad memory between the two of us and one that I hope he has forgotten in his current state.

Ironically, my father would like the grounds outside Pleasant Valley Acres as they are quite nice and very well groomed and cared for. The original building has been there for over a hundred years, and many of the trees have been there even longer. Winding paths throughout the area are surrounded by weeping willow trees and tall stately oaks. This was one of the rare examples of the actual place looking better than the brochure. It was a crisp fall day, and Chuck and I were walking the snaking trails behind the main building with my father. My mother decided to stay behind to talk with some of the caregivers.

"Still got a pretty good step in those old legs, Pop," Chuck said as he strolled next to my dad, holding his arm in his.

"Harrumph," my father retorted.

"Nice day," I said, thinking that I might as well have said "Get me the fuck out of here, I am so uncomfortable."

"Yeah," Chuck replied, thinking the exact same thing. We walked in silence for the next five minutes, and then my father stopped abruptly and looked at Chuck.

"Let me talk to that one," my father said bluntly to Chuck.

"What do you mean?" Chuck replied, and then my father looked directly at me.

"What?" I said, feeling intense terror start to shoot throughout my entire body.

"Oh. I get it. You mean . . . you want to talk to Neil alone?" Chuck remarked.

I motioned desperately for Chuck to stay, but Chuck quickly let go of my father's arm. "Okay. Sure. I will, uh . . . I'll go skip some stones over at that pond and let you two girls talk."

"Harrumph," my father replied affirmatively.

"Okay then," Chuck said to us both. "I'll meet you back at the . . . the main . . . place."

And with that, Chuck practically jumped up and ran for joy with his newfound freedom. My father and I turned around and started walking slowly back toward the main building.

"So . . . nice day, isn't it?" I asked, looking anywhere but toward my father. It was official. I had hit a new low in the conversation, so we just walked along and said nothing for a few more minutes. Unlike Chuck, I was uncomfortable taking my father's arm as we walked, so I ambled beside him, kicking rocks, leaves, sticks . . . anything to justify not being directly next to him. After something slightly less than an eternity, we got back to the main building and my father stopped ten feet from the bottom step leading to the entryway. He didn't move a muscle for another minute as he stared straight ahead at the doors.

"You okay, Dad?" I asked as my father continued to stare blankly ahead.

"Your mother thinks I'm . . ."

I walked up to him and with every ounce of courage I could muster. I took his arm and led him over to a nearby bench. He sat willingly, and I sat next to him, releasing his arm at the first opportunity. But as soon as I did, my father grabbed it back.

"I need your help, son," he implored. My eyes opened wide in amazement as my father had never uttered those words to me before. I was even more startled to hear him call me "son."

"Yeah, Dad?" I replied, hoping I could actually do something to help him. He shifted uncomfortably on the bench and then blurted it out.

"I need to get out of here."

My father continued to look aimlessly ahead, but these were the first real words he had spoken to me in years. And he was asking me for my help. I didn't know what to say, but I had to say something.

"I don't blame you," I said sympathetically. "What can I do, Dad?"

"I don't know," my father replied as he hung his head.

I couldn't help but reach over and put my hand on his back. But the right words were still not flowing into my mind.

"Mom says this place is really expensive."

Dang it. *That* was the best thing I could come up with? I knew I had blown it by mentioning the expensive part, but it was true. There is a huge irony to life, career, and money. You save and save and save for retirement, and then this is what you spend it on? A place that leaves you with little hope and no dignity. It was pathetic, and I agreed with my father. He needed to get out of there, but where would he go? Who would take care of him? Clearly my mother couldn't do it anymore. I might not even have a place to live soon myself. And Chuck was worthless in this department. No, my father needed to be in a place like this, but I had to think of something else to say soon or this small "moment" with my Dad would be forever ruined. Then it came to me. The perfect thing to say.

"You deserve better than this, Dad."

With that, my father looked up and into my eyes and actually . . . smiled. He grabbed my hand and stood, and we walked slowly back up the stairs and into the building. When we got into the main hall, my mother saw us and rushed over to take my father's arm. Chuck followed her. My dad continued to hold my hand.

"Well, well. What did you two young men talk about out there?" my mother said, knowing my father was in one of his rare good states.

"We were just talking man-to-man stuff," I uttered proudly with a smile.

"Yeah, sure," Chuck retorted. "He probably wanted to hear that chocolate cake story again."

My mother scowled at Chuck and we all began walking down the long corridor.

"You want to watch a game on television, Dad?" Chuck asked excitedly. "The playoffs are on. Gotta see the Hawks get clobbered again. You want to?"

It occurred to me immediately that Chuck was jealous of me for whatever it was that had happened out there. I knew it wasn't much, but it was something. For some reason, my father chose me to talk to about his desire to leave. Between the time machine, my mother correcting me about the graduation, and this, my father suddenly didn't seem like such a horrible guy anymore. I let go of his hand as Chuck grabbed his arm.

"My work here is done," I whispered facetiously to my mother.

"Looks like his medication finally kicked in," my mother responded, popping the pride balloon that was still floating over my head. My face drooped, and my mother smiled and grabbed my arm. "I'm just kidding, Neil. Come on. Let's all go get something to eat. I can tell you had a moment out there and I want to hear all about it."

"It wasn't a moment. I don't know. It was just . . ."

"I know. Come on," she stated proudly. "I'm buying."

As we walked, my mind raced with thoughts of how I may have misread my father many times over the years. We were different, but that didn't necessarily mean . . . wrong. He was my father. He probably did the best he could and gave me everything I needed to get to where I am now. I guess you could say he literally made me what I am today. Wait a minute. Despite this nice little stroll with my father, I was a total mess. But was that his fault or mine, or a combination? Over the next few weeks, I would discover the answer to that question.

Chapter 20

TRUST MAY BE THE MOST VALUABLE COMMODITY ON EARTH

My brother and I did not talk much on the long ride back to Cleveland. We had done most of the normal "remember whens" (reminiscing about girls, sports, music, college, girls) on the drive to Louisville, and now my mind was fixated on what to do about Rachel. It had been six days since I got her note, and I had not even talked to the kids since then. I had sent her a text telling her that I was going to go visit my parents, but she did not respond. My instincts were usually good about when to ask for forgiveness, but I was not sure what to do this time. Missing the birthday party was bad, but I concluded it was just a last straw for Rachel. Her resentment had been growing for quite a while and I think she was hoping I would do something like that eventually. And it was inevitable that I would.

When we pulled up to my house, my brother asked if we could go get a beer that weekend and I agreed. I got my bags and went into what now seemed like a very empty and sad house. I sat down in one of the comfortable chairs in the living room and fell asleep. It was the type of deep sleep where you feel you are so tired, you might never wake up. I had been asleep for about an hour when I heard a vehicle coming into the driveway. Could it be Rachel and the kids coming back home? I got up and went to the front window only to see a delivery van parked in the drive. It was one of those overnight delivery services, and I quickly became afraid that it could be Rachel sending me divorce papers. Could our marriage really be over that fast? I wasn't ready to see what might be in the package, so I grabbed my jacket and started off down the street toward the green door house. When I walked inside, it appeared to be the same as always. Except for one thing. The broken doorknob was now taped back on the door with some gray duct tape. All the other times the knob had sat on the floor, but there it was . . . back where it was supposed to be. I entered the front room and called out for Dobie.

"Hey, buddy," I said, not knowing what else to call him. "Buddy" seemed right to me. "Hey, let's get on with it. I'm ready to . . . where are you?"

As I peered down the dimly lit hallway, Dobie suddenly appeared at my side. It startled me so much that I jumped back and bumped clumsily into a wall and almost fell.

"Why do you do that?" I asked as I regained my balance. "You could kill a guy my age sneaking up on them like that."

"Sorry," Dobie said as he motioned for me to take a seat on the couch. "So you think you are ready for this again? So soon?" he asked as we both sat down.

"I . . . think I am. I need to do something. I'm scared my wife just sent me divorce papers."

"Oh no," Dobie replied. "Let's hope that isn't the case."

"I was too scared to open the package, so I came here. I want to keep doing this until you let me go somewhere good. Some place or time that makes sense and helps me."

"Well then, I think I have just the place. Do you trust me?"

I had to think for a minute before responding.

"Not really. But what choice do I have?" I stated emphatically.

With that, Dobie got up and led me to a door on the left side toward the back of the hallway. I stepped carefully into the stairway and felt the dampness of the air on my forehead. I began walking slowly down the stairs and eventually found myself in a room with no windows or doors. When the darkness diminished, I was lying on an operating table. I was awake but was starting to feel drowsy. This was the place Dobie picked for me? A happy place? I don't think so. The room was full of nurses and doctors rushing about in preparation for something. Then it hit me. This was the day I had my hernia surgery. It was fifteen years ago, so I was thirty-five. Rachel and I were still in a newlywed phase even though it had been a few years since we had tied the knot. My surgeon came over to speak to me as I fought off the urge to fall asleep.

"We're going to get started soon," he said as he pulled the surgical mask over his mouth. He continued to speak through the mask. "We will get you to sleep here soon. Afterward, you will wake up in the recovery room and we will talk. You will be feeling much better very soon, Mr. Moreland."

"Thanks, doctor," I stated weakly. "But why am I so tired? I feel like I'm about to pass out."

"We gave you a little something in the IV to relax you, that's all. You were pretty freaked out back there."

What he meant by "back there" was that I had been worried about being put under and I told them that I wanted to see the credentials of the anesthesiologist. I had just read a book called *Coma*, and the patients in that book were given sleeping gas for simple procedures, but they never woke up. The hospital executives then sold off their vital organs for huge profits while the barely living bodies hung in a huge refrigerated warehouse. It was a good book and an even better movie, but it forever made me nervous about anesthesia, doctors, and hospitals. To be a for-profit entity would naturally cause the hospital administrators to think of new and better ways to make money, right?

For example, why do so many drugs that we use for depression or anxiety need to be taken regularly for the rest of our lives? It seemed to me that the goal was not to cure, but to addict or create a dependency to the drug. I had the same issue with the psychiatric field. If they really did their job and cured the patient of their mental malady, then the patient wouldn't need to come back. No, they had to get the patient to think that psychoanalysis and regular visits were the only way to cope with the world. So, yes, I was a bit paranoid about the hospital's actual motives and the doctor knew it. Nevertheless, I had a very painful hernia and it needed to be fixed.

"We'll have you out of here in a jiffy," the doctor said cheerfully.

As I lay there waiting for the mask to be placed on my face, I remembered that Rachel was waiting for me in the next room. She was so supportive of me back in those days. There were no kids or stresses yet to keep us from giving each other what we needed to be happy. Plus, Rachel worked full-time back then, and she got a lot of her social needs met from her coworkers. By the time she got home from her job, she was just as tired as me and didn't need to "vent" about or discuss her rotten day. No, back in those days, we happily coexisted. We went to movies whenever we could, and we could laugh over dinner instead of correcting the girls or breaking up arguments. There was no hectic schedule to discuss and no agenda. It was fun, and we seemed to really be "in love." At least I thought we were.

In addition, as a couple, I knew I was the one that married up as Rachel was very pretty. But one thing that I didn't expect was that Rachel seemed to get even prettier as she aged. While I have gained twenty pounds and a double chin, she has stayed trim and is even more stylish today than when we met. One of the nice things about having some money as older adults is the ability to spend it on ourselves in ways that we couldn't when we were borrowing everything just to get by. As soon as we started having more money than it took to pay the mortgage and food bills, Rachel put some of her excess portion into clothes, hairstyling and other beauty procedures. The cost was in the hundreds per month, but I didn't care. I thought it was money well-spent as the pampering made Rachel happy and, in general, when she was happy, I was happy.

At the time of my hernia operation, she was thirty-five and we were working on starting a family. As I laid there waiting, I wished that I could pop up from the bed and run out into the waiting room to hug and kiss her. She was worried for me and she would go on to take very good care of me for the next two weeks while I healed from the surgery. I continued to dwell on Rachel's beauty while I watched the surgical team do all their busy work in front of me.

"We're going to give you some drugs now, Neil." the surgeon stated. I nodded and suddenly a rush of euphoria came over me, and then a sense of warmness flowed through my entire body. In those days, this type of operation was much more serious than it is today with all the laser and arthroscopic advancements. Back then, they cut into you with a scalpel, and I had a pretty bad hernia to boot. I was going to be in the hospital for three days as opposed to the three hours it would be today.

As they placed the oxygen apparatus on me, I tried my best to be conscious of the exact moment when I would fall asleep. But this is one of the things in life that is literally impossible to do. Like sneezing with your eyes open, it cannot be done. No one remembers the moment they fall asleep or they would probably be too awake to actually fall asleep. I waited for that moment, however, and was determined to get as close to it as I could. But this time I did not go to sleep as the surgeon suggested I would. This time, I was fully aware that I was being cut into and could do nothing to stop it. I tried to yell out, but I couldn't make a sound. Oh my god. Was I in a coma? Is this what a coma was like? Would I forever be trapped in this dark place with no way to communicate with the outside world? What would I do if I was trapped inside this motionless body forever? I wouldn't even be able to watch television. This was horrible. I tried to scream out but opened my eyes when I heard a familiar voice.

"Wake up, sweetie."

I blinked to adjust to the light, and then Rachel's face came into focus.

"Everything went fine," she said, smiling down at me. "You gave birth to a sweet little six-ounce hernia. I put him in a bottle to take home with us."

I looked around the hospital room and then back up into the eyes of my (once) adoring wife as she gently brushed the hair away from my face.

"Do you feel okay?" she asked in a whispered and loving tone.

"I feel like garbage. You ... you look great," I said, although uttering each word felt like I was pushing a razor blade down my throat. I guess it was the effect of the anesthesia, but I didn't feel that bad considering I had just had a knife stuck into my gut.

I couldn't help but wish I had used an adjective better than "great" to describe my wife's appearance, but I was still a bit groggy from the operation. I remember vowing at one point in my life to work at increasing my vocabulary. I was a good reader and decent writer, but I was not confident enough to use words that were not in my normal every day vocabulary. I also used to say "shit" way too often. But *shit* is a word that can be used in so many interesting ways. Yet, when the girls came along, I had to break that *shit* thing off and I did.

"You don't look so bad either ... considering," Rachel responded with a smile.

I wanted to jump up and kiss her. I wanted to tell her how sorry I was for the next fifteen years. Here was this pretty girl who had made the decision to marry me. She could have had so many other guys—probably much better guys—but she chose me. And she chose me when she was still so young. She gave up the rest of her life ... for this? For me? How could I have let her do that? If I really loved her, as the Sting song says, I would have set her free.

"Do you need something? Something to drink, maybe?"

I nodded, and Rachel took the pitcher of water from the bedside table and poured it into a real drinking glass. It had been ages since the last time I saw a real glass and not some plastic thing with a bending straw. She placed the glass carefully to my lips, but the water proceeded to flow down the front of my chin and onto the bedsheets. Okay, now I see why they give you a bending straw in the hospital.

"Oh gosh. I'm sorry, Sweetie."

Those words. Those words had not been spoken in so long. Rachel, for all her goodness, was not an apologetic person. It was difficult for her to admit to any wrongdoing, especially with me. And she had not called me sweetie in at least ten years. Boy, those were different times. What had caused the distance to build between us? It would be easy to think it was the kids, but it couldn't be. We wanted those girls so badly. It was one thing that we both agreed on one hundred percent. And when we learned that we couldn't have them biologically, we went right into the adoption process without hesitation. In fact, there was a conference on adoption that we went to where the panel discussed all the different options for the prospective adopters. There was domestic, international, open, closed, partially open—even surrogacy was discussed. We sat through three hours of the seminar without speaking a word to each other, but when we were walking to the car to leave, my wife looked at me and smiled.

"China," she blurted out as we approached the car.

"Agreed," I said back as if we were so close to each other mentally that we could speak in code.

No, we wanted those kids and loved them with all our hearts. They were our focus and the best part of life for both of us. I knew that. The challenge was figuring out why we had fallen so far apart despite the gift of such amazing children. They should have completed our dream. And a dream it was. We had everything on the surface. We had our families. We had enough money not to worry about the necessities. I still worried about money at times, but that is what the man is taught to do, right? But deep down I knew we would always be okay financially. So what was it that drove us apart?

"Are you okay? I'm going to go downstairs and get you some magazines," Rachel said as she got up and smoothed out the wrinkles on her dress. "You still like reading those celebrity gossip papers like the *Enquirer*, right?"

I nodded, and she winked at me. Then I got it. That was the reason Dobie took me here. To remember how things worked when they worked for me and Rachel. I could use this to figure out how to make things right between us. But as Rachel opened the door to leave, an attractive young nurse walked in. Her skin was tan, and she had the shiniest brown hair I had ever seen. The contrast of the dark hair and the all-white nurses' uniform was striking, but her face and smile were also intoxicating. She was tall and skinny and had large breasts which were accentuated by a uniform that was at least two sizes too small. She looked like a girl from one of those bachelor party movies, and I was instantly turned on.

"It's time for your medication, Mr. Moreland. You've been naughty as I see that you've used up all of your pain drip," she said as she tapped on the tube that led into a taped needle on my hand. The morphine drip was an amazing convenience. Back in those days, you could just push a button when you wanted—or technically "needed"—more painkiller, and the morphine would flow into your veins with an immediate impact. It felt so good to me that I simply left my thumb on the button until the flow would stop. I am sure they metered it out somehow, but I loved the feeling. The pretty nurse then unhooked the bottle and placed another one on the top of the IV stand next to the bed.

"You need to take this only when you need it . . . for pain only," she said as she adjusted my sheets. "I'll be back in a few hours to check you. Just push the orange button if you need me."

"Can't you stay just a little longer?" I implored to her with a flirtatious smile. "I'm really sick and I'm scared I might not make it if you leave."

Yep. Pathetic. That was how I flirted. Normally, I would try to use humor and self-deprecation to lure women into talking with me. I have always enjoyed the thrill of talking to pretty women and believed it was harmless as long as Rachel didn't see it. I watched every step the nurse took as she left the room. The fantasy part of my brain was already at work with what she would do the next time she came in. She would dim the lights as if to help me sleep. I would complain about a cramp in my side and she would massage it. As she rubbed me, we would look deeply into each other's eyes and the urge to kiss would overwhelm both of us. But wait, there I was fantasizing about this stranger while my loving wife was off to get me something to read to help pass the time. What the heck was wrong with me?

My doctor then entered the room and he was holding one of those silver chart folders like all doctors do on TV. You know, like the ones on *M*A*S*H* that are metal and all official looking. The doctor opens it and checks off a few things before hanging it back up on a bedside hook. It was classic "doctoring" from the 70s and 80s. All you needed to look like a qualified physician was to carry a stethoscope and one of those metal charts. Feeling disappointed in the collapse of my nurse fantasy, I must have looked like I felt worse physically than I really did. The doctor put his hand on my forehead and opened the chart again.

"I don't like the way some of your levels are looking. Might be some elevation from the anesthesia, but I want to check it out. I'll be back in an hour and we'll run some tests. You sit tight, all right?"

I nodded my head nervously as the doctor left the room. Anesthesia? Tests? Was my worst fear coming true? Please, God, tell me it isn't so. Tell me I am not going to die from some bobble-headed anesthesiologist's mistake? Was this to be my own version of *Coma*? But wait, I was feeling okay at that moment and certainly was well enough to let my imagination go wild. That nurse was so pretty and—wait—could I have seen signs of interest on her part?

As I lay there on the bed resuming my fantasy, I should have concluded that the nurse that came in was not nearly as pretty as Rachel. I should have also assumed that she was a giant bag full of craziness that she would unleash on any unsuspecting fool who dared to flirt with her. So why do we let our minds go to places like this? Somewhere inside of me, I feared that I would have acted on that fantasy if the nurse had really showed interest. But why? Why break that sacred bond of trust? Why would I throw it all away? I have learned since then how important trust is and that it should be guarded at all costs. Here I was in the best of situations. I had an attractive wife who was smart, not crazy, and nice to me. I had been given such a gift of companionship and yet, there I was, thinking about some pretty nurse and what I would do if given the opportunity. And in the years to come, that opportunity would arrive, and I would indeed risk throwing it all away.

Chapter 21

A WEDDING VOW IS A ONE-WAY STREET

After reliving the hospital experience, I found myself sitting on the couch again across from Dobie. It was a sunny day and the sun shone through the window onto Dobie, creating a bit of an aura around his spiritual body. I sat up and wiped my eyes.

"Well, that was interesting," I remarked sleepily.

"She sure was pretty, wasn't she?" Dobie responded.

"Who do mean? The nurse or Rachel?"

"Rachel, of course," he said emphatically.

"Oh yeah. Of course. Rachel. She was. I mean, she is. Wait. Do you get to see all that goes on when I'm on one of these ... trips?" I asked.

"I only see what you want me to see or what you want me to know."

"You meant like reading my mind?" I queried in frustration at another statement from Dobie that made very little sense to me.

"It depends really. You see, I must realize some of what is going on, so we can talk about it afterward. If you want to, that is," Dobie replied in a soft tone.

I stood up and tucked in my shirt and looked out the window as a car passed.

"Dobie? Can I ask you something? Can I ask a favor?"

"Of course, Neil. I'm here to help you."

"Well, if that is the case, can you . . . I mean, if you can . . . can you help me get my wife back? I know I screwed up a good thing and I want to . . . get her back."

Dobie sauntered over to the couch and sat down next to me as the sun continued to shine on his face.

"Let me put it this way: All of this. Me. Everything here is meant to assist you," he said while crossing his legs and uncrossing them.

"So, tell me then, what do I do? That last trip . . . to my operation. I get it. It was early in our marriage and I loved her. She loved me . . . and we let it all slip away. Right? So what do we do now?"

"You are still married to her, Neil. She is your wife. She's not gone from you completely . . . not yet."

"What do you mean not yet? What do you know?"

"I know that as long as you are still married, there is a chance. Have you or Rachel found someone else? You haven't, have you?" he asked.

"No," I said, but I had a secret and it was then I began thinking that Dobie probably knew. He knew about my lie—the lie that broke her trust of me.

"Good," he said. "As long as you have fidelity and trust, you can still make it work."

Okay, apparently, he didn't know.

"What do you mean exactly?" I asked again while trying to look as innocent as I could.

"I mean trust. Do you trust each other? Haven't you been faithful?"

Okay, maybe he did know.

"If you mean, have I ever cheated on her, then . . . well, come on. You know everything. You know I haven't."

"Are you being honest with me?" Dobie responded.

"Oh, you mean that one time?" I snickered. "Oh gosh. It was like three years ago, and it was nothing. And the girl, she kissed me. I didn't start the thing. And we didn't do . . . well, everything. We just kissed a bit . . . and . . . shit. Sorry, I mean, shoot. It didn't mean anything. I told Rachel about it right away and she forgave me for it . . . after a few weeks. She told me I had to end all communication with that girl and I agreed. But you know that already, don't you?"

"Fidelity is a lot more than remaining loyal to her physically, Neil. It is about dedicating yourself to someone else's happiness."

"Okay, fine. So I have some selfish tendencies. So what? Doesn't everyone?"

"Let me ask you this. You love your children, right?"

"Of course."

"If Mary or Jessica asked you to be there for them, to listen to them, if they had a rough day, you would do that for them. Correct?"

"Sure."

"If they ever got into trouble—legal trouble—or if one of them got pregnant or arrested, you would support them, right?"

"Of course. One hundred percent! Where are you leading me here?" I stammered. "All I did was make out with some stupid girl at a holiday party. I was drunk. She was drunk. And I told you. I told Rachel about it right away."

"I know you did. But it didn't stop there, did it?"

"Yes, it did. I never touched her again. I swear," I replied emphatically.

"Wasn't there an issue with your e-mail?" Dobie asked.

Now, I knew it was true. He knew everything, so there was no reason to hold back anymore. And I guess I was finally ready to admit to my real crime.

"Yeah."

I ran my hands through my hair and leaned in closer to Dobie to begin my full confession.

"There was more. Guess I should have cut off the e-mails too. The girl. The one I kissed. She got transferred, to Seattle . . . but she kept writing to me."

"And you wrote her back or e-mailed her, as they say now?"

"It was kind of fun," I confessed. "It was innocent enough at first. She had a crush on me. And she was cute . . . and she was in Seattle now. So I thought it was okay or safe to, you know, e-mail her back. We were just discussing her life out there mostly. No one was getting hurt."

"I may have to disagree with that."

"What? Who got hurt? It was just some innocent exchanges and Rachel should never have found out."

"But she did, didn't she?"

"She snooped into my computer and . . . she saw the e-mails from her. It was, well, you can see. She did the snooping. She caused all this. I didn't mean it to hurt her."

"But you did hurt her and worse, you broke the bond of trust. And she only looked at the computer because you gave her reason to. You left evidence that you were not done with it. She wasn't snooping. She was looking for reassurance and found out it was still going on."

"Jesus!" I shouted. "How do you know all this? Can't I do anything right? I may not be perfect, but I'm not a beast either. I never meant to hurt anyone, especially Rachel."

"I know, but you hurt yourself and your family with your dishonesty. That's why I asked what you would be willing to do for your children? Wouldn't you be willing to do the same thing for your wife?

I didn't mean to, but I actually paused a moment before answering "Of course."

"She is your wife, Neil. The family starts and ends with that relationship. You know that right?" Dobie questioned.

"I know it now, that's for sure," I replied without pause this time.

"Even the innocent flirting, as you say, was doing your relationship harm. The best thing that could have happened was for you to get caught."

"You're wrong, Dobie. I was just having a little fun, and there certainly hasn't been much of that the past ten years. She was interested in me and I wouldn't have done it if the girl was here . . . in town, you know? It was safe with her out there on the West Coast. And I was bored, and Rachel was totally caught up in her own life and raising the girls. But it doesn't mean I'm not dedicated to my family. I do. I am. I always will be."

"So, you say you are one-hundred percent dedicated to their happiness . . . to making them happy, safe and secure. Rachel too."

"Yes."

"Do you remember your vows, Neil?"

"Vows to what?"

"Your marriage vows," Dobie clarified.

"Sure. Everyone knows them. Wait. I . . . think . . . I do. The honor-and-obey stuff . . . till death do us part. All that?"

"It is a vow, Neil. Not a statement or even a promise, but a vow to love and protect in times of sickness and in health. You vowed to give that to Rachel."

"Okay, so I vowed. So what? So do half the people in this country and they still cheat. They still get divorced."

"But have you delivered on those vows, Neil?"

"Marriage is a two-way street, isn't it?" I probed. "Isn't it? It isn't just about her, is it? I have my needs too. And my needs, well, I have needs too."

"The vows aren't about your needs, Neil. They are about hers."

"But she makes the same vows?" I stated and stood up to exaggerate my point. "You are talking crazy shit here. It's about both of us making each other happy, protected and all that, right?"

"I think we need to go back to your wedding day, Neil. You need to listen to what you said. Let me take you back to that moment when you promised her to—"

I raised my hand to cut Dobie off.

"I don't need to go back to that day . . . or to . . . any other day. Shit. I'm outta here. This place is full of shit. You are full of shit. I'm just a human being. I'm not perfect. All you do is bring back painful memories and make me feel like shit. I'm done."

For some reason, my problem using the word *shit* had just resurfaced in a big way. And with that, I left and started marching back toward my house. With each step, my anger seemed to build. What did he mean vows are a one-way street? Shouldn't there be compromises on both sides? As I slowed my pace, I started to think back on my wedding day. Rachel was literally glowing and so happy that her cheeks literally looked sore from smiling so much. I know that on the wedding day, the girl is fulfilling her childhood dream, but it was a special day for me too. My friends were all there and I was doing something good and I was proud that she chose me. But like all good things for me, I managed to find a way to let the memory of that day become tarnished too.

Our wedding was in the summer and the church we chose had no air-conditioning. During the ceremony, I was sweating so much that I had to wipe my face off every few minutes with a handkerchief. If it kept up, I would soon be sweating through my outer jacket. I knew this was an offshoot of my fear of public attention. I was horribly embarrassed by the sweating. When the ceremony was over, some of my friends joked that I was crying at the altar due to the use of my handkerchief. I wasn't crying, but it probably looked like I was wiping away tears instead of sweat. Again, I was embarrassed at myself and that is usually what I thought of when I thought of our wedding day.

As I walked along towards home, I slowed a bit while the wedding-day memories continued to flood my mind. Could it be that I had not paid close enough attention to the words I was saying? Maybe I should go back and relive that moment—the moment I committed myself to her during that service. Maybe Dobie was right. It wasn't about our oath to each other; it was about my oath to her. Each of us had our own path to take with this marriage and I needed to focus on mine. I promised to love her and protect her and now she was gone. I must have done something wrong to screw things up so badly. It was time to fix that.

It occurred to me that this exact moment could be the turning point for me. It was an epiphany of sorts. I decided right then and there that I would indeed return to the green-door house. I would go back to our wedding day and I would listen and listen better this time. And maybe it would help me figure this out and get Rachel back. So I turned the corner with determination, but as I turned, I felt a sudden stabbing pain in my chest. Within seconds, I hit the pavement with a resounding *thud*. The description of a knife in the chest is what some people say a heart attack feels like. This one felt more like a spear through the heart and lungs and up my throat. As I crawled to the curb, I concluded that this was likely to be my last moment on earth. I cried out, "Please don't take me now. Please, God. Don't take me now!" And strangely, I do remember the exact moment before I passed out. Perhaps it was because this time, I was not coming back.

Chapter 22

IS IT A SIN TO WANT TO BE DEAD?

There is a very wide expanse between being dead and wanting to be dead. When I woke up in the hospital, I was very much alive, but I almost wished I wasn't. I was in more pain than I could imagine. My head hurt, my chest ached horribly, and it took all my effort to keep my eyes from tearing up each time I took a breath. I seemed to be hooked up to every apparatus imaginable. I had two needles in my arms, conductor patches on every conceivable part of my body, and there was a tube up my nose. I hadn't seen the doctor since I woke up, but at least six nurses had come in to change bottles and check monitors. Not one of them said a thing to me.

I could tell I was in critical condition as they didn't even bother turning off the lights in the room I was in. In the bed to my left (it was a shared room) was an old man who hadn't moved since I got there. I knew he wasn't dead as there was a little accordion-looking thing that kept going up and down, so I had to figure that was him breathing . . . or something breathing for him. Like he old man, I couldn't really move as I was held down by so many tubes and cords. I had no idea of the time or date. When your body is in tremendous pain, your brain compensates as much as it can, and I went into a trance-like state where I just wanted to lay there and let my body rest.

After who knows how long, I tried to reach for the remote to the television, but it was too far for me to grab. With nothing to read and nothing to do, my mind ruminated on how bad my life had become and how miserable I was. My wife and kids were gone. I was totally sick of my job. And this heart thing hurt so much, I wasn't sure I wanted to be alive. I couldn't help but think that if this was my time to go, so be it. I was ready.

Just then, the door to the room swung open and in came a doctor holding, yes, one of those metal clipboards. He was a large man in his late forties and he seemed to really know his way around the monitoring devices as he read and made notes from them. He barely looked up from the clipboard as he maneuvered his way around my bed. He flipped to another page in the chart and I wondered if he even considered that a living human being was laying there in front of him. Had he acclimated so much to this world of treating illness that he no longer saw the body in front of him as a real person? He flipped another page and still said nothing. If I was up to it, I would have gotten out of the bed and walked out. But given the pain I was in, I just tried to wait patiently for him to say . . . something. He finally did, and it was not what I wanted to hear.

"Well, well, Mr. Moreland. That was a very close call, and we aren't out of this yet. I don't know how you made it. I really don't."

I was thinking but didn't say *Nice to meet you too, asshole.* But instead I just laid there, silently hating him.

"The Thrombolysis wasn't enough. I'm still very concerned here."

Throm-fucking what?!! I thought as the doctor continued to write on the chart.

"We've got several tests lined up for you today and tomorrow. But the blood work shows that you have experienced a very serious heart attack. We must have had blockage in at least two of the main arteries. Like I said, I don't see how you made it. You are a very lucky man."

And with that, he turned and started to walk out of the room. The flower vase was out of my range to throw at him, so I shouted out the best I could as he started to open the door. But all that came out of my mouth was a gasp followed by a horrible hacking cough. The doctor turned around purposefully as if to ask *What did you say? Can't you see that I'm a super important busy person?*

I swallowed hard and attempted to speak again and this time, I could muster a few words.

"Is that it?"

"Is what it?" the doctor smugly replied.

"Can't you even take two minutes to talk to me?"

I could tell at that point that the doctor seriously considered leaving, but some small bit of morality kept him standing at the door.

"Very well then. What did you want to know?"

"Well, how about what happened to me? Who found me? How did I get here? What can I do about all this pain? And ... and ..."

As the last word left my mouth, the sheer power of the pain caused me to feel faint and I stopped in mid-sentence. The doctor's face quickly changed from indifference to one of concern, and he rushed to my bedside and took hold of my wrist.

"I'm sorry. I didn't know you were in such pain. Let me get you something for that."

The doctor pushed a button on the bedside remote and a nurse appeared at the door.

"Nurse, I need two milligrams Dilaudid. Stat."

"Yes, doctor," the nurse said as she disappeared through the doorway.

"The drugs will help you. In the meantime, I'll get those tests moved up."

"Okay," I said, although I wasn't sure if it was audible.

"You just need to rest, okay? We can give you something to help you sleep. If you need it. Just push the button and I'll have some medication lined up for you."

Even doctors must be reminded to be human occasionally, and this was one of those times. His face changed from that of a robotic medical engineer to a real person as he looked me over. To say anything else at that time would have ruined a positive moment for both of us. He seemed to sense that too, so he smiled and said nothing else before he left. Within fifteen seconds, another young nurse came rushing in. She had in her hands a syringe, and she inserted it into one of my two intravenous lines.

"This will help you feel a lot better, Mr. Moreland. I'm sorry I didn't give it to you earlier, but you were sleeping."

"That's okay," I said, already feeling the impact of the drugs in my system. It's remarkable how well these drugs work as the flow of the narcotics into my brain was as soothing as getting into a hot tub.

The nurse smiled back at me and tugged on a few of the other lines and looked at the monitors again.

"Can I ask you something?" I said while cringing to indicate that I was still in some pain.

"Sure," she replied. "Do you need something else?"

"No. It's just ... well, is there anyone out there? Has anyone come to see me?"

"Oh, of course," she said smiling, and for a moment I held out hope that Rachel was there in the waiting room.

"Your brother came by yesterday. You were still sleeping, but he stayed for an hour anyway. He sure is something. He had the entire staff in stitches. He's so funny."

That was Chuck. There I was near death, and he found it to be an occasion where he could show off his comedic skills and flirt with some cute female nurses.

"Is your brother . . . is he?"

"Is he what? Gay?" I responded. The Dilaudid was now kicking into full gear.

"Oh, I'm sorry. I didn't . . ."

"He's single. Divorced, I mean," I said.

"Oh. Well, I just thought . . . I'm sorry I asked."

"No. No. That's okay." I grinned. "He's a good guy. And you are definitely his type."

The nurse smiled back, and I realized that she was probably no more than twenty-five years old. Almost half Chuck's age. *How sad,* I thought, but the pain medication was working so well now that I didn't even care that Chuck was the center of her attention and not me. But I did care that Rachel had not stopped by. Surely someone had told her I was in the hospital. To me, that was a sign that our marriage might really be over. She probably wished I had died. That would be easier than the difficulty of going through a divorce.

So, despite the pain-killer eliminating most everything I had felt before, I was back to thinking that maybe I should pray that God take me; that I should just unhook these wires and tubes and let this be the end. I had nothing to live for really. My life had been a total waste to this point. I had done nothing but screw it up and had nothing to show for it. I looked over at the cord leading to the heart monitor and considered pulling the plug from the wall. As I reached over to see if I could theoretically do it, I knocked a water pitcher over onto the floor. With that, three nurses came rushing in to see what had happened. One of them picked up the plastic pitcher and put it back on the nightstand. Another got a paper towel to clean up the water that had spilled on the floor. Another checked the tubes and tapped on the clear bottle sending saline into my system. All the while, not one of them said a thing.

Chapter 23

A Hospital is a Great Place to go to get Sicker

"Neil. Neil. Can you hear me? The girls are here. They want to see you."

The sound of that voice was so familiar, but I was in the middle of a deep sleep and I was dreaming about being on a beautiful white horse that had wings. I was flying through the clouds and the air was so cool and comfortable. The feeling of flying in dreams is so surreal and peaceful. The closest thing to it in real life is swimming underwater. I hated to leave that idyllic scene, but the voice persisted.

"Neil. Wake up. The girls need to see you."

I opened my eyes to see Rachel standing near the bed, but not close enough for me to reach out and touch her. I smiled and motioned her over, but she remained a few feet away.

"Let me go get them, okay? They are so worried. I want them to see that you are alive, okay?"

It was clear that Rachel's primary concern was for our kids. Not for me.

"Okay," I replied sleepily as Rachel turned to leave.

"But wait ... when ... when did you get here?" I asked pushing the wires and tubes out of the way so I could sit up a bit on the bed. Rachel made an instinctive move to help me but stopped. I knew from that motion that she simply couldn't allow herself to show any emotion or compassion toward me. I have seen enough relationships break down to know that when one of the parties involved finds some level of peace apart from the other, they don't want anything to spoil that.

It killed me to see her showing a lack of empathy toward me, but I deserved it. Still, there I was in a hospital, having almost died from a heart attack, and yet she couldn't allow herself to come near me.

"Rachel," I uttered quietly to demonstrate my willingness to allow her the space she needed. "I only wanted to ask you, before we see the girls, how are you? How have you been?"

Rachel took a half-step farther away in response and said nothing. She wiped her forehead with her hand and fiddled with her purse. I could tell she did not want to be in the room with me. I motioned for her to have a seat in the red-cushioned chair next to the window, but she didn't move. She just stood there.

"Look, Rach. Don't worry. I know you need to be . . . that we need to be apart right now. I'm not . . . I'm just asking you about you. I've done a lot of thinking since getting your note and . . . and I just want a chance to be with you . . . alone, so we can talk."

As the words left my mouth, I knew they were not the ones she wanted to hear. Heck, even I wouldn't want to be subjected to talking with me in this state and in this room. The sterile environment of the hospital room was only ripe for cold and emotionless thought. The nurses and doctors had proven that very clearly in the week I had spent here. I was now resigned to getting the interaction I needed from an occasional stop-by from Chuck. My mother had told me that she would come to help me back into my house when they discharged me, but that did not appear to be happening anytime soon. All the doctors had told me over the last few days was that it looked like I would be needing some kind of bypass procedure. They didn't think I was quite strong enough yet to go through such an intense surgery, so I was simply waiting it out in my hospital bed.

"Neil, I'm sorry you got sick. Not that I didn't . . . I mean, the way you eat. You should have known it was coming."

"Wait. What do you mean? You think I meant to have this . . . thing happen?"

"You think sugary cereals and Diet Cokes are a good healthy diet? For God's sake, you don't even take vitamins. And when was the last time you did anything good for your heart besides walking that stupid dog? Come on."

Okay, so that was how she felt. Here I am about to have my guts cut open and my wife is going to blame the entire thing on me. Like I was just troubling or inconveniencing her with my heart attack. I knew if I spoke what I was thinking at that moment, it would do irreparable damage. So I tried to think of something to say to change the subject, but the silence was indicative of my disdain for her comments. I reached over for the glass of water on the bed stand and, in the process, I jerked out one of the tubes that was stuck in my hand. Blood began to shoot out of the open wound and Rachel immediately sprang into action. She grabbed the glass and set it on the table. Without hesitation, she took a linen cloth from the cafeteria tray and applied pressure to my hand to stop the bleeding.

"Nurse. Nurse. Can you come in here please?" she shouted. It was the first time in years that I had seen Rachel do what she does best. She was and still is the master of the crisis. Whenever one of the girls had an accident or hurt themselves, she seemed to know exactly what to do and precisely what to say. It was remarkable to watch her in action.

"You need to keep the pressure on this," she said as she realigned the wires and tubes that had become entangled. "I don't know how they expect you to exist like this with all this stuff on you. It's just not human."

Rachel grimaced briefly as she let go of the napkin to see if the blood flow had stopped. It had not. I could tell that she loved being a caretaker, even if it was for me. As crazy as this sounds, this was one of the best moments in the last few years of our marriage.

Eventually, one of the male nurses came in and took over holding the napkin to my hand. He then continued to untangle me from the mass of wires and tubes. Within a minute or two, the IV tube was back into place and the bleeding was stopped. The nurse re-bandaged the connection as I pushed my back upward on the bed to sit up straight. By then, Rachel's face was back to the stoic expression she had worn when she first arrived. And she again backed her way toward the door.

"Maybe this isn't the best time for the girls to see you. With all that blood and all. How about I bring them back tomorrow or the day after that?"

"Okay. Makes sense," I said as it did make sense. "I'll make sure they clean all this up."

The male nurse looked up at me as if to say *That's not my job* and went on with his current duties. Rachel turned and walked out without even a smile or a nod of her head. Nevertheless, I was encouraged by what had happened. For a moment there, she seemed to care and that felt good. It felt really good. I just had to figure out how to get that feeling back into her long-term.

"Please try not to jerk the tubes loose again," the nurse said. "If you need something, just ring the buzzer next time."

As the nurse uttered these words, I wondered if I could take out one of the long needles in my arm and stick it into his boney ass. For those who have not spent more than a day in the hospital, let me inform you that it is a terrible place to go when you are sick. Or another truism is that a hospital is a good place to go to get sicker. Not only are the staff overworked and overstressed; they eventually start to smell like antiseptic. And their personalities become antiseptic too. But rather than dwell on the negative, I vowed to use this as a major motivator to get well and stay well. As a lot of people say after their first heart attack: "This was a wake-up call!" But only the lucky ones who survive the heart attack are able to say that. For some reason, I was one of the lucky ones.

Chapter 24

AIRLINES AND HOSPITALS ARE A LOT ALIKE

I was quite relieved when they told me that I was finally strong enough to have my operation. To me, it had begun to feel like a delayed flight where the airplane staff tell you nothing and expect you to stay stuck in your seat, happy, polite, and relaxed even though your plans have been completely crushed by some disgruntled mechanic who forgot to tighten a screw. Air travel and hospitals are a lot alike in that way. The customer has become the victim of a poorly run organization where the financial goal is to avoid bankruptcy while offering minimal service. I hate airlines as much as the nurse who came in to start the preparation for my operation.

"Don't eat anything after noon today and you can't have nothing to drink after ten p.m.," she said harshly.

"Okay," I said as she literally jerked a pillow out from under my head. This was typical of the behavior the nurses displayed during my lengthy stay. No empathy or sympathy at all. It was all business and often it was done with little attention to detail. In short, they were as sick of me as I was of them.

"The doctor wants you to get to sleep before nine tonight. I can get you something to help you sleep if you need it."

The smallish nurse with black curly hair then proceeded to mercilessly rip a bandage off my arm.

THE HOUSE *of* REMEMBER WHEN

"Yigza!" I howled.

"Sit still, please. We are going to have to redo all the connections."

The nurse then began to pull off the tape on my arm while holding the tubes running into my hand. I watched and tried my best to keep her from hearing any sign of my significantly low pain tolerance.

"Ouchie ouch," I murmured as she pulled and tugged on a particularly stingy strip of tape. *Ouchie ouch?* What an embarrassment I was to myself.

"I'm sorry if this hurt, but I have a job to do here. If you will just sit still, I'll just be a minute more."

"Oh, okay," I said with a smile, hoping to ease the tension a bit as she ripped off another bandage.

"The worst part is done," she said as she began putting new bandages back on my arm.

"Excuse me," I said as politely as I could, "I was wondering, I mean ... can I ask you a question?"

The nurse looked up in surprise as if she had not been engaged in real conversation by a patient in years.

"What?" she asked curtly.

"Keep in mind, I am just generalizing here. I don't mean you, specifically."

The nurse's face began to form a scowl and I knew I had better get to the point and fast.

"Can you just tell me why you people hate your job so much? I mean, why would you want to be a nurse if you don't enjoy helping sick people?"

The words were out and there was no way I could take them back or rephrase them. I had no idea what to expect in return. And with that, the nurse ripped off another piece of tape.

"I thought you were done," I cried out, but it was as if I had said nothing.

"I don't hate my job," she said angrily. "I just hate doing it sometimes."

I pondered what she could have meant by that, but I couldn't help but take it personally. That is just the way I am built.

"So is it me? Or just people like me? I mean, did I do something wrong here?"

"I really can't say," she said, looking to see if there were any other fragments of well-adhered tape that she could rip off my body.

"Look," I said, trying to look sincere. "I want to get out of here as much as you want me out. I just wished you—I mean, the staff, could be just a little bit, uh, nicer."

As the last word of that sentence rolled off my tongue, I saw the facial expression of the young nurse totally transform. It went from emotionless to relaxed and then almost to a pleasant expression. As she smoothed out one of the new bandages, she reached over and put her hand on my shoulder.

"I'm sorry. I know we aren't always the most compassionate. It's just . . ." She paused.

"What?" I said, not realizing that her answer was going to change my view of hospital care for the rest of my life.

"I guess I get mad at people," she said while adjusting my pillow.

"Like me? What do you mean?"

"I'm sorry. But I get angry with people . . . yes, like you . . . for letting things get so bad."

As I let those words sink in, I knew there was great truth in her statement. She continued.

"Most of the people we see in here are sick because they didn't take care of they body. They eat too much. They don't exercise. Hell, we get smokers in here who want to blame the cigarettes for their lungs being all black and messed up. Damn, they're the one that stuck that smoke in they lungs. Hell, they did this to they-selves."

The profanity and alternative grammar only seem to enhance the truth of what the young woman was saying. She picked up some paper cups and towelettes and disposed of them while she continued. She was on a roll now and there was no stopping her.

"And we also get people in here that don't need to be in here. I had an old woman on the floor last week that didn't have nothing more than a common cold. But she took a bed and was here complaining and ringing her buzzer every damn minute for over a week. I mean, come on! That bed could have been used for someone that was really sick. We was practically full and there are really sick people that need beds. But she rang that buzzer for this and for that, while other sick people waited for us to get to them."

I nodded in a fashion that I knew would encourage her to speak on.

"And then we get patients who are really sick. Cancer. Leukemia. Nasty stuff. Little kids that don't know what they got, but they're dying and . . ."

The young nurse wiped her face as if to wipe away the entrapped emotion that she guarded so carefully.

"They ... many of them end up dying. Right here. We try to help them, but they die anyway. Poor little kids. Young men and women too. They get sick and leave they families behind. It's tragic."

It was apparent she could no longer control her emotions, so she quickly reached for a Kleenex as she sat down in the chair next to my bed. I wished that I had the strength to stand up and hug her or at least put my arm around her to comfort her as the tears trickled down her face. Little did I know that my innocent little question would unleash years of pent-up emotion that was finally finding its way into the world. I knew from her reaction that many of the other staff had to do the same with their emotions. If you let every child who died and every young mother who suffered pain get into your system, you would not be able to do this job long term. The emotional toll would be too much to bear.

"Wow. Thank you for sharing that with me," I confessed, hoping to help the woman feel better. "I had no idea. But I think I understand better now."

"Yeah, well, it's my job," she commented as she stood up to leave. "You need anything else?"

"No. I'm good. Thanks again," I stated while pulling the sheets up to my chest.

"Good luck tomorrow. You just ring me if you need something. I'll be right outside," she said with a crooked but beautiful smile.

As I lay there thinking of the way I had treated my body, I knew she was right about so many things. How had I let this happen to me? It was twenty years ago that my doctor told me to watch my weight and my triglycerides. I didn't know exactly what that term *triglyceride* meant, but he prescribed some statin medication that I was supposed to take every day for the rest of my life. I had only filled the prescription once and had never taken it. And there I was at age fifty with my first heart attack. But I had survived. I had another chance at life. I had the chance to treat this body better and to get it into shape. As I drifted off to sleep, I made a plan to get back to the gym. To get healthy. I just hoped that this painful experience and the words from that beautiful young nurse had done enough to scare me straight.

Chapter 25

IN THE SIMPLEST TERMS, PRAYER WORKS

When they came in to wheel me out to the operating room, I was ready but nervous too. I had spent the night before writing down all the things I wanted my kids to know in case something bad happened to me during the operation. The letters were short, but I poured out my love onto paper. As I sealed the notes into hospital stationery, I wondered how many other patients had written their last words in the very same way. We have so many opportunities to tell people that we love them, but we put it off or we regard it as "overkill." We don't want to diminish the impact of the words, but I wonder if it is possible to tell someone that you love them ... too much?

As they rolled me down the corridor to the operating room, I watched the mass of people walk by on either side. The thought then hit me that there were a ton of sick people in this world. This place was literally a city of professional people all here to care for those of us who needed their help to stay alive. Like the young nurse had said the night before, some of us deserve to be here. But many had no choice and were only here to ease the pain of their disease or malady until they passed on. I really had not thought about the possibility of truly dying before that moment.

"Good morning, Mr. Moreland."

I looked up to see my surgeon staring down at me as they transferred me from the stretcher onto the operating table.

"Not so sure it is a good morning for me," I said chuckling. "Let's hope it is."

"Oh, don't you worry. We will take good care of you," the doctor said with a smile.

As he said this, I realized that this guy was almost young enough to be my own son. He was in his mid-thirties, but I must have looked old enough to him to be a "mister." In my head, it always shocked me when people addressed me as if I were an adult. Some people seemed to be born to act and speak like adults. I was different. I was born to have the mind of a teenager and that is how I perceived myself. For some reason, eighteen was the age where I simply seemed to stop maturing.

"The procedure itself should only take about five to six hours. You will be in recovery for another few hours after that. But it will be a while before we will know that the operation was totally successful. I assume you have made all of your arrangements just in case."

I hadn't. The thought did occur to me briefly when I was signing all the paperwork required before the surgery. You can't not think about it when you sign a paper saying that the hospital has zero liability in the event that they screw things up. I wondered if my family knew how serious this was. My mother had arrived the night before, but she only told me positive things like "You are going to be a new man after this" and "I just know it's all going to go well" and "The Cleveland Clinic is the best there is." I appreciated her support. It wasn't that I wanted sympathy. I truly didn't want to be a burden on anyone. But I did imagine a scene where my mother, Chuck, and Rachel were in the waiting room, crying and praying that my surgery would work. But in reality, I wondered if Rachel would even show up at all.

"You will need to sign a few documents here," said a woman in gray business attire. She was holding a clipboard, but it wasn't one of the metal ones. I guess only doctors get to carry those. "You do have a living will, correct?"

I nodded affirmatively, even though I wasn't quite sure what that meant. The term seemed like an oxymoron to me. Rachel and I had seen a lawyer once, years ago, about doing our wills. I remember him mentioning the term, so I figured we must have one. But I had to face the truth: I might not wake up from this thing and I was not ready for that. It seemed my only thoughts at that time centered on regrets. What the heck good had I ever done in this world? Had I ever done anything to really help anyone? If I was to die, the obituary would probably read: NEIL MORELAND. A WASTED LIFE.

"Sign there and there," the hospital staffer said as he pointed to the spots and I obliged.

The doctor then moved toward the front of the table and looked down at me with a peaceful smile.

"The anesthesiologist will come and talk to you in just a minute, but I was wondering if you would mind if we meditated together before we begin?"

I looked up in surprise. He wanted to meditate? Say what?! Didn't he have enough confidence in what he was doing? What the heck good would meditating do? I suddenly felt very uncomfortable, and it must have been obvious to the surgeon.

"It's up to you, but it is my custom to ask all my patients if they would like to meditate together before surgery. Call it prayer if you like, but I find it helpful. Would that be okay with you? Or I can just do it on my own."

Whew! I was relieved that this was just some sort of pre-game ritual and not a plea for God's help that he clear the correct artery. I believe in God, but it wasn't God who would be cutting into my chest. It was this guy. With that, he grabbed my hand and closed his eyes. The nurses and other staff went on with their duties as he spoke.

"Lord, you perfectly made Mr. Moreland and you made these fine vessels leading to his heart. I know that you can help me fix them. So I'm asking You to help me apply all my skills in doing this surgery and that it be a success. In Your Name, we pray."

I didn't close my eyes while he spoke, but I did feel a sense of warmth come over me when he was finished. I concluded, however, that this was probably just my body blushing from the awkwardness of praying with all these other people watching. He was also holding my hand, which is a form of personal space invasion for me. In fact, this type of hand-holding was a "deal-killer" for me in choosing a church. If the church service required public hand-holding during prayer, then that church was not for me. I was not necessarily against prayer in schools or other public places, but I did feel like it had to be fair and non-intrusive. This doctor's meditation thing was borderline for me, but at least he asked me first. I was glad he gave me the choice.

"We will start you on some drugs now to relax you," the anesthesiologist said. "Then I'll explain how the anesthesia works."

Suddenly, the movie *Coma* came back into my head again, but the Demerol relaxed those fears before they could take root. As my mind and body became sleepier, I started to wonder again who might be there for me when I got out of this, or if I got out of this. Was Rachel out there? Did she care if I lived or died? What were my kids thinking? Did my father understand any of what was going on with me? Things were becoming a little blurry now from the drugs, but I could see the staff's faces looking down at me. All of them seemed to be confident and I could somehow sense the surgeon was smiling beneath his mask.

"I'm going to start the anesthesia now," one of the doctors said as she applied the mask to my face. "You just want to breathe normally and watch my face. When I tell you, I want you to count backwards from ten to one, okay?"

I nodded and thought that I would once again try to notice the exact moment that I drifted off. As they repositioned the mask, I thought that it might be worth it to sneak in one last prayer. "God," I said, "sorry to be such a screwup."

"Okay," the anesthesiologist said, "you can start counting now."

"Ten," I uttered, and that's the last thing I remember.

Chapter 26

WHO WOULD CHOOSE AN APPLE OVER A HO HO?

"Don't you have any cereals with marshmallows?" Chuck asked me as he looked through the pantry in my kitchen. He had just come back from his two-hour swim and that is when Chuck would be so hungry, he would literally eat almost anything. My mother was staying with me while I recovered from the surgery, but she spent just as much time waiting on Chuck as she did me. I had been home over a week. The surgery was successful, but it sure didn't feel like it to me. My entire body was sore, and I had so little energy that it was a colossal effort just to get up to go to the bathroom.

"You know he can't have any junk like that, dear," my mother said to Chuck as she wiped off the kitchen table with a dishrag. "We need to set a good example. Eat some of that healthy fiber cereal. I bought some yesterday."

"I'm not eating that crap. I had a bowl yesterday and couldn't make it an hour without a colon explosion. No thanks."

"Well then, have something else. I bought apples. Have an apple."

My mother was a huge fan of apples and throughout our life, she had always suggested apples whenever we asked for a snack. To this day, I hate apples for that reason. When a teenager comes home from three hours of basketball practice, an apple just doesn't supply the same satisfaction as a box of Ring Dings. If I could have ever been satisfied with just one Ring Ding at a sitting (would that be a "ring" or a "ding"?), I'm sure my mother would have been more apt to buy them. But whenever we had anything sugary and good like Ho Hos or my favorite, Marshmallow Pies, I would eat them all within the first few hours of the tasty treats entering the house. When it came to chocolate cake, marshmallow filling, and icing, I was an addict. And the entire family knew it.

"Who ate all the dang Ho Hos?" my father once shouted out from the kitchen. "For heaven's sake, we just bought them."

Upon hearing my father, I shoved the last bite of my fifth Ho Ho into my mouth in hopes that he would not catch me in the act. The plastic wrapper remnants of my sin in the trash were bad enough. In the days living alone before marriage, I knew not to bring this type of thing into my apartment. If I did, I would eat sugary crap and nothing else. I had also been given some great advice that you should never grocery-shop while hungry. The result would likely be that my house would be filled with frozen fried chicken dinners and rocky road ice cream. On the other hand, if I ate a nice big meal before grabbing a shopping cart, I would choose healthier fare like vegetables and frozen lean dinners. I liked the lean dinners, but the problem with those three-hundred-calorie frozen meals was that I needed to eat three of them to get full.

Yes, I have an eating problem. And the only way to handle it in my past was not to have the stuff in the house. When the kids came along, I had to resist eating their lunch foods which were right up my hunger alley. Cheetos, corn chips, and miniature candy bars were all stuffed into the cabinet next to the stove with a large yellow sticky-note that read *Not for Neil*. Rachel knew that I was basically a kitchen "grazer" and I would come down at any hour of the day or night to forage for food. In the last few years, the food I was supposed to eat was relegated to a small section of the cabinet with healthy things like low-fat granola bars, fiber cereals, and probiotic cookies. Good thing they had preservatives in them as they just sat there collecting dust month after month.

When we were leaving the hospital, a nurse handed my mother a list of "heart-healthy" approved foods. After two weeks in the hospital, I had lost fifteen pounds. At 185, I was within only ten pounds of my doctor-prescribed weight of 175. I knew I could get there, but it would take discipline and a change of mind on what was truly right to put in my body. The nutritionist at the hospital also suggested that I start by charting everything I ate. At the end of each week, I was to weigh myself and note the weight in a logbook. The goal, she said, was not to get skinny, but to get healthy. She had seen enough anorexia and bulimia to scare her straight on what was truly healthy.

"We are all meant to be the shape God intended us to be," she told me. "If Karen Carpenter had accepted that she was meant to have a larger-than-average size ass, she would still be here today, singing like an angel."

I noted that this reference to Karen Carpenter meant that the nutritionist was stuck in the '60s and '70s music era just like me. In my opinion, all the good music had been written by the Beatles, the Rolling Stones, and Bruce Springsteen. Publicly, I have stated many times that there was no reason to listen to anything else. Secretly, I was also and continue to be a huge Monkee's fan, but I don't admit to that publicly.

"Let's go out. Fuck, I can't eat any of this shit," Chuck grumbled as he slammed the pantry door shut.

"Theodore, please!" my mother scolded.

"Sorry, ma. Hey, Neil, you up for going to Chili's or someplace like that?" Chuck inquired as I shifted my weight on the couch to get more comfortable.

"No thanks. You guys can go. I'm okay here by myself."

"Neil, the doctors said it was good for you to move around. Come on, let's go to that Italian place in Shaker. I'll treat."

"Shit yeah," Chuck replied in delight that his mother would again be paying for his next meal.

"Okay," I mumbled as I pushed my sore body off the couch and sat up. I knew she was right and I thought that maybe moving around a bit would help me to feel better. My chest hurt. My legs hurt. My arms hurt. The doctor told me that my operation had been more difficult than they expected. They cleared two complete blockages and put a stent in to help prevent another episode down the road. I knew I was lucky. My cholesterol was so high that they really didn't have a chart for people like me. Most people like me were already dead.

"I'll get dressed and we can go," I mumbled again as I struggled to stand up. My mother rushed to my side and took my arm as I walked to the stairs. "I got it from here, Mom."

"Are you sure? I can help you get dressed," she said lovingly.

"Ha!" Chuck blurted out from the kitchen. He had found a bag of mini-marshmallows and was popping them into his mouth ten at a time. He continued to laugh as he strolled into the living room.

"I got this, Mom. But thanks," I said.

I put my left hand on the banister rail and grabbed it firmly to pull myself up the first stair. The pain felt as if I had someone sticking ice picks into every joint in my lower body. I struggled to push myself up another step. I got to the third step and felt the first drop of sweat trickle down my forehead and onto my white T-shirt. Then another, and then a steady flow of sweat dripped off my forehead and onto the carpeted stairs. I looked up and saw that there were exactly eleven steps left to the landing . . . and another eight steps up from there to the second floor. I knew I couldn't make it, but I didn't want to look as pathetic as I felt to my mother and brother. As subtly as I could, I turned around to head back down the three steps and saw both of them staring back up at me.

"What?" I said with exhausted breath.

"What the fuck, bro!?" Chuck stated through a startled expression.

"I'm fine. I think I better just go back to the couch for now, though."

"I'll make you something. It's too soon. You just go lay down," my mother said as she pushed Chuck out of her way to help me. Chuck didn't know what to do or say, so he did nothing except stare at me as I made my way back down the three steps.

"Fuck," he said again as I passed him on the way to the couch.

Chuck's three favorite words were *shit, fuck,* and *bro,* and he seemed to say them at least ten thousand times a day. (He probably replaced *bro* with "dude" when talking to his friends.) I appreciated him coming over most nights as that meant he was leaving his wild teenage kids alone in his house on nights they weren't with their mother. Probably not the smartest move, knowing Chuck's kids, but he seemed okay letting them fend for themselves. I moved slowly back to the sofa where I laid down gently on my side. I knew then that I had a long way to go to full recovery and that, for a while, it would be a struggle to do even simple things. It dawned on me too that I would need help and it would be far more than my mother could provide. She had my father to deal with and Chuck—well, try as he may (and he didn't), he was more of a burden than a help. I had to think of how this recovery could work for me. I would need a driver, a cook, a nurse, a house cleaner... I needed a caregiver. I needed Rachel.

Chapter 27

THE DIFFERENCE BETWEEN BEING ALIVE AND DEAD IS LIKE COMPARING THE OCEAN TO A DESERT

It was the end of the third quarter of a JV basketball game and I was, as usual, sitting on the bench pouting that I was not out there on the floor. I was a good basketball player, but I tended to play too recklessly at times and that got me in trouble with fouls and with my coach. He didn't like my all-out style of play or my hot temperament. But that was me, and in my mind, the excess energy made me better. To my coach, it made me un-coachable. While my football coach and baseball coach (the same guy) really liked my spirit, this older coach did not. To demonstrate his disdain, he once inserted me into a game for a single foul shot. That's right. I was replaced before the shooter shot his second free throw. Basically, I was inserted to do nothing except be embarrassed in front of the people in the stands. I didn't even look at the coach when I walked back to the end of the bench. To me, this was the ultimate embarrassment and as a fifteen year old, I took it like a very young immature kid. I pouted.

But one of our games that year was a rout and I figured that I would get some playing time when he pulled out the starters. With six minutes left in the fourth quarter, that happened. I got into the game and I figured there would be just enough time for me to get a few points and possibly a rebound or two. The JV coach then made a curious decision. There were three other sophomore players on the

JV that also sat on the varsity bench. And since this game was such a blowout, he allowed them to leave to go to the locker room early to be with the varsity squad who would play next. That left exactly five players so the remaining five of us were in the game until the end.

Part of the basketball skill set that I had developed in earlier years was the ability to dribble the ball equally well with either hand. As a kid, I used to walk the dog holding the leash with my right hand while dribbling a basketball with my left hand. Learning to dribble with both hands made it easier for me to get the ball up court, and I liked being the player that did that. I had a good outside shot too and bringing the ball up court would put me into a position to be open for a long shot as the ball got passed around. Despite all this, the coach usually inserted me into the second forward spot, which meant I was to simply position myself for picks and rebounds as the others passed the ball and tried to score. That wasn't much fun for me, so in this game I decided to give the coach an exposition of my well-honed dribbling skills and took the inbound after the next opponent score.

There I was proudly dribbling the ball up court. The game and score were well in hand, so I didn't think the coach would mind that much. Even the referees seemed to be showing some mercy on our opponent by not calling as many fouls on them as merited. As a result, one of the opponents began to flail his arms at me to steal the ball and with a hard whack on my right arm, he did just that and went down to the other end to score. My coach glared at me as I prepared to take the ball out again.

"No foul? Really!?" I barked at the referee while taking the ball out again.

While this was not enough sass to be given a technical foul, it was certainly enough to leave the referee influenced negatively toward me. The coach motioned for me to get the ball up court faster and I began the process again . . . and again the opponent flailed his arms at me, hitting my wrists, shoulder, forearm, hand, and every other part of my upper body. With no one near to pass to, I simply muscled through his battery of fouls and heard the referee's whistle. Thankfully, I assumed they were finally going to call a foul on this spastic dork. But that was not what happened. The referee turned to the scorer's table and began to say my number. The foul he was calling was on me ... not the dork.

Holding the ball firmly in my hands, I yelled again towards the ref, "You've got to be kidding me? You called that on me?!"

With that, my opponent looked toward me and laughed obnoxiously enough to push the red temper button in my brain. He would have to pay. And without hesitation, I took the basketball and began to whip it toward him. It was on the path to hit him in the chest when a terrible, terrible thing happened. The referee was returning to the court to resume play and he traveled into the path of the thrown orb. To my horror, the ball hit the referee right in the side of the head.

Everything then in the old gymnasium seemed to go into slow motion. The boos from the stands echoed as I watched the referee make the motion to throw me out of the game. I didn't look at the coach as I walked toward the bench, but I could hear him shouting something about forfeiting due to having only four players left. What could he want with me? I knew I was wrong, but didn't he know it was an accident to hit the ref and not the opponent? In my simple fifteen-year-old mind, this was a huge distinction, but it wasn't to the coach. When the boos subsided, he took me by the upper arm and walked me toward the gymnasium exit.

"Get out of here," he said as he pushed me on toward the double doors. "You have played your last basketball game at this school."

"Who gives a shit?!" I responded as he slammed the door behind me.

He was right. I never did play basketball for the school again despite, in my mind, being good enough to start on the varsity team. It was a "life is not fair" learning that still seems grossly wrong to me to this day. Aren't kids (especially fifteen-year-olds) allowed to make a mistake? It was just another humiliation for me and, right or wrong, I still think that other kid deserved to be clobbered with the basketball. The one positive from this entire situation was that my father was not there to witness it. Finally, I could chalk up a positive from him not ever attending my games.

It was another week before I could do much of anything besides sleep, eat, and go to the bathroom ... and do my crossword puzzle, of course. And between the pain medication and the pure boredom of lying on the coach, I had been hoping to get back to the house with the green door. I had gotten so bored lying around that I even began to detest watching television. At one point in my younger life, I told a friend that I loved television so much that as long as I had cable TV, I would never be bored. On most days, a few hours of television at night didn't seem too much at all to me. In fact, I often fell asleep with the remote control in my hand, hoping to get as much programming into my brain as I could before I conked out. This recovery experience had changed my perception of television completely. I was sick of it.

Other than a few good rerun programs, there was nothing but trash on TV. The ridiculous was now newsworthy on stations like CNN and Fox. Even my beloved Sports Center station started to appear to be nothing but trivial fodder on spoiled rotten prima donnas. And it repeated over and over. Did we really care that much about what stretching exercises Tiger Woods does to prepare for a round of golf? At one time, I did. I don't anymore. In fact, I didn't want to know anything about Tiger Woods or any other athlete. Were they really our heroes? Was LeBron James's decision to go play somewhere else so important that we burned his jersey in effigy? To spend that much time perfecting a golf swing or dribbling skills instead of living a life suddenly seemed ludicrous to me.

It was a rainy morning when I was finally ready to try to walk all the way to the green-door house on my own. If I could make it, I decided that I would ask Dobie to take me back to Jessica's baptism. I wanted to relive a time when my family was still a family. It was only six years ago when we baptized Jessie, but so much had changed since then. My father was now ... not all there anymore. My marriage was no longer intact. But on that baptism day, things were still mostly good, and the future seemed bright. All I had to do was not screw up my life after that. I thought that going back to that event might help me figure out a way to do things better.

When I finally arrived at the house, it appeared different. For some reason, the home seemed even older than before. A new layer of dust had settled on the floor and window sills. The stairs seemed to have aged too as the bright wood trim seemed to have become dull. I entered the house slowly and peered down the hallway.

"Dobie. Hey, Dobie. I'm back."

Like a wisp of wind, Dobie breezed in from around the corner. He seemed to have a very pleasant expression on his face.

"How are you, Neil? Are you better?" he asked.

"I'm good. Had a heart attack," I said matter-of-factly. "But you knew that, I'm sure."

"Whoa! No, I didn't! I'm so sorry."

"Yes, you did. I'm onto you now. Admit it," I responded.

"Okay, I knew, but it lessens your perception of my concern not to see my shock and surprise, right?"

"They said I was lucky to survive. I'm lucky to be alive."

"Well, we all are," Dobie responded. "So what brings you back?"

I was just about to tell Dobie my idea of the baptism when an interesting thought hit me.

"I was going to ask you if I could go back to see my kids' baptisms. First Jessie and then Mary's."

"Sure ... uh, we can do that," Dobie said in a curious tone.

"What?" I asked when I saw Dobie's puzzled expression.

"It's just. Isn't there another idea you wanted to explore?" Dobie responded.

How the heck did he know that? I hadn't told anyone about this idea and I wasn't even sure it was worth bringing up. Nevertheless, I decided to at least broach the subject.

"I do have one, but it's a little crazy. You might not like it."

"Okay then. If that's the case, then let's send you back to the baptisms," Dobie stated as he turned to walk down the hallway.

"Wait," I blurted out toward him.

"Yes?" he responded.

"You know ... you know what I'm thinking, don't you?"

"I might, but I don't advise it," Dobie said emphatically.

"But is it possible?"

"Is what possible?"

"Uh ..." I paused as I tried to think of a good way to phrase my inquiry. I had thought about this while in the hospital, but the rules of this house were still not entirely clear to me.

"Go on. You can ask me anything. Did you have a specific time in mind that you want to revisit?" Dobie asked.

"I do," I responded. "But, uh, can you? I mean, can I ... is it possible to go ... forward? Forward in time?"

Dobie laughed and sat down on the couch and crossed his legs in his usual manner. He continued to chuckle to himself while a bead of sweat dropped from my brow.

"You are really something. You know that?" Dobie replied with a chuckle.

"What? You said I could ask you anything. And then you laugh at me?"

"No, no. I'm sorry. That was not what I thought you were going to ask. I'm not as sharp as usual today, I guess."

"What did you think I was going to ask?"

"Oh, I thought maybe ... no. I think I get it. This makes sense. You want to go forward to see where all this is leading. So you can try to change how you act today to prevent ... well, to prevent things from going badly. The Christmas Carol story. Dickens, right?"

"Exactly! So is it possible?"

"It is," he said. "But again, I don't advise it. You see, time is not linear the way it seems to you today. Time just ... well, time flows in a big circle but it all moves in one direction. Life is life and your life is your life. And it all exists at once—past, present, and future. They are all in the same place in a way. Going back is one thing. You can relive or get a new perspective on a past event. But going forward is different. You will be experiencing it again, but in your mind of today, it will be the first time. And that dissonance can cause a great deal of anxiety. I think you would be better served going back. In fact, I was thinking we could go back to—"

"No thanks," I interrupted. "I almost died from this heart thing and I want to know what is going to happen to me. I want to go forward."

"But I just explained. If we put you in some situation that hasn't happened yet, it can be difficult for your mind to comprehend. In other words, experiencing something again that you haven't experienced yet, in your mind is, well, it is a problem."

"Then let's not go to a time when I was living."

"What?" Dobie said with surprise.

"I want to go . . . no, you are going to say no."

"Wait. Ask me," Dobie implored. "I think I know now where you are going with this."

"Okay, here it is. I want to go to my own funeral."

Dobie blinked several times and then closed his eyes for a few seconds.

"Wow. Again, not what I was thinking. We can do that, but I don't think that is a good idea either. I really don't."

"But I almost died a few weeks ago. And I want to hear what people would say about me after I'm gone. I've always imagined that God allows us to watch our own funerals. I just want to see mine . . . before, well, before I actually die."

"I don't know."

"Come on, Dobie. So far, all you have done is show me painful things. Can't we try? I want to see who shows up and what I was able to make of my life. This way, I could know what I still need to do. I could prepare myself to do better today."

"Well, maybe."

"Just let me try it, okay? Maybe you can just let me take a quick look, and then you can pull me back if it doesn't work. I just want to know. It will help me to know."

Dobie paced the floor of the hallway and then turned and nodded his head.

"So we can do it. You'll let me go there?"

"Come this way," Dobie said as he walked me down the hallway to the last doorway on the right. He opened it slowly and then paused. "Are you sure?"

"I'm sure," I said as I walked in front of Dobie to begin the descent down the stairs.

The air in the stairwell was damp and cool. As I descended, I felt a chill and then my body lost all normal sensation. In fact, within seconds I was without any senses at all—sight, smell, or hearing. I knew immediately that I had made a major mistake in doing this. I tried to turn around to run up the stairs, but I couldn't. And then my mind and body suddenly went blank. All the pain, pleasure and emotion that you normally feel as a human being was absent. I felt nothing in my hands or feet. I tried to look around to see where I was, but there was nothing there. Then it hit me. I had asked Dobie to take me back to my funeral, but I hadn't thought this through. In each of the other events, I was able to relive the experience in my own body at that time. But in the case of my funeral, my body would be . . . dead.

I couldn't remember if I had chosen in my will to be cremated or simply stuffed and buried in my dead skin. But it probably didn't matter. If I was dead, then I was dead. I wondered if I was in my coffin. I tried to scream out, but I couldn't. All I knew was that there was nothing more to me or to my life. The absence of life is quite remarkable. The difference between being alive and dead is like the ocean and desert. Life in the water is full and rich and moving. The desert is hot and dull and . . . lifeless. I knew at that moment that I did not want to be dead. No matter how tough life was, I would much rather have the chance to do something, to change or to try to be better than to have no chance at all.

Then a wind blew, and a leaf fell to the ground and somehow, I was there. I was in the wind and I was part of the leaf. The sun shot a piercing ray of heat into me and I wilted. I felt the process of chemicals changing and moving in me. Cells danced about and absorbed nutrients. I was an atom and then I was a nucleus and then I was the cell wall. Was this the sensation of being conceived? Another breeze came, and I was in the clouds. I had always wanted to feel the feeling of flying and here it was. I was in the breeze and it was taking me wherever it wanted. I enjoyed the peaceful feeling of that moment, but it ended all too soon when I entered the water. In the water, I was immersed in coldness. I wanted to shiver to relieve a portion of the reaction associated with the cold, but I couldn't. I didn't know if this was existence in some elementary way or if this was non-existence. Either way, it contained an emptiness that words cannot describe.

And then suddenly, I heard a sound like a *pow*, and I was back on the couch in the old home. Dobie was sitting in the chair across from me.

"What the heck?" I shouted as I tried to shake the horrible empty feeling out of my head.

"Sorry. I tried to warn you," Dobie responded. "You couldn't go to your funeral because you were not there. You see?"

"You could have told me that. What the heck was that? Where was I? Was that heaven or hell?" I asked angrily.

"I told you," Dobie replied. "I warned you not to try to go forward. It just isn't . . . it shouldn't be done."

"I didn't want to be dead. I wanted to hear what people said about me. Thanks a lot!" I shouted into the air.

"Our time alive is what matters, Neil. God wanted to show you what life is like without Him in it. It is emptiness, Neil. You need to ask Him to..."

"Geezus!" I cried out, trying to shake off the remarkably bad feeling that had overcome my entire body. It is impossible to fully describe the feeling of being dead. It was way worse than any hangover or sickness. It was a mental pain that must be something like the feeling of being locked in a dark prison cell or in solitary confinement. Or in a coma. The absence of life is nothing like I had imagined. It was not the heaven people described in those near-death experiences. It was nothingness. It occurred to me that it could have been that I was in hell, but who knows? Could hell be the lack of life? Or the lack of love and emotion? Do people that murder and commit heinous crimes live with this feeling while still walking the earth?

"I gotta go," I blurted out as I stood up to walk toward the front door.

"I'm sorry. I tried to explain to you. But maybe if you could just ask God to ..."

"Forget it, Dobie. I'm done here. This really is my last time. Have a good ... life, if you are even alive."

I went out the door and walked back to my house in a drizzling rain. As I headed home, I vowed that I would never enter that house again. Each experience had been worse than the one before. Wasn't this supposed to help me? I had always thought that I would eventually "get it," and that this house would hold some special secret for me that I could use to carry on. But if there was a secret to it, I wasn't in on it. In my opinion, the green-door house hadn't helped me at all. When I got closer to my home, I saw a car in the driveway. My freshly repaired heart started to race with excitement, which scared me. It was Rachel's car.

Chapter 28

THE TRUTH MAY NOT ALWAYS BE EASY, BUT IT IS FAR BETTER THAN A LIE

I entered our home to find Rachel standing in the hallway holding a large green duffel bag.

"Hey, Rachel!" I exclaimed, trying to hide the hopefulness that she had come back to stay. "Are you here for a visit or are you . . . leaving?"

"I was . . . I am. I tried to call first. I didn't expect you. I'm sorry. H-how are you feeling?" she asked.

"I'm doing better. Lost fifteen pounds so far," I stated proudly while patting my stomach. "Course, it was mostly from the crappy hospital food. But I am going to try to keep it off. Haven't had a Diet Coke in a month."

"That's good. I'm glad," Rachel responded nervously. "Listen, I was just gathering some things, but... did you get the package I sent you?"

Oh shit. The package. I had completely forgotten about it. Or more likely, I had blocked it out in fear that I wouldn't like what I found inside.

"I haven't opened it," I confessed

"That's okay. You probably shouldn't open it just yet, anyway. I'm not sure you are ready. How about this? I'll let you know when to open it, okay?"

That sounded weird, but at least it didn't sound like the package contained divorce papers.

"Okay, so I guess then . . . you aren't . . . going to stay?"

Rachel's expression began to sour as she turned and walked into the family room. I knew it was the wrong thing to do, but I couldn't resist. I ran to her and grabbed her arm. I wanted to hug her so badly. I attempted to pull her toward me, but she jerked her arm away violently.

"Don't," she said, dropping the green bag in the process.

"Why not?" I shouted. "Why are you doing this to me?"

"What do you mean why?" she said as she turned to face me. "Don't you have any idea what you have done?"

I tried to maneuver myself so I could look directly into Rachel's eyes. She was trying to hide the tears that were trickling down the side of her cheek.

"Please, honey," I begged. "We have to talk about all this."

"I tried to talk to you a hundred times, Neil. But you were always too busy doing your crossword. Or there was a game on. Or you just didn't feel like it."

"I'm sorry," I said as I tried to grab her arm more gently this time. I desperately wanted to pull her closer, but I knew that was the wrong thing to do. Seeing her tears made me realize what a complete fool I had been. Here was this attractive woman that I had been so lucky to have agreed to share her life with me—and I had blown it. I had hurt her, lied to her, and damaged her. Each tear that ran out of her eyes was a painful stab in my gut. It was a reminder that you can never take love for granted. It is such a gift. And there was nothing I could do now. You can't apologize for years of neglect and abuse. I had never meant to hurt Rachel, but the mental damage I had done was quite evident. She had taken all that she could take, and this was the end. She needed to be done with me and for the first time, I felt like it truly was too late.

"I'm sorry. I'm just really, really sorry," I said as I let go of her arm.

"Just let me leave. I need to go. Okay?" she pleaded as she wiped her cheek again.

"Okay," I said as gracefully as I could. Rachel picked up the green bag and started toward the door. I watched her as she walked away from me for good.

"Can I just tell you one thing?" I asked while fighting off the urge to cry myself. "Can I just tell you that I know I was wrong? That all these years of us, just existing, were my fault."

Rachel slowed her pace toward the front door, and I knew this was a chance for me to get in, perhaps, one more apology.

"And that girl from that party meant nothing. Those e-mails were just stupid of me."

Rachel stopped and sighed with exasperation and I knew instantly that this was the wrong thing to bring up. But she wasn't leaving just yet, so I continued.

"I can't explain it, Rach. Maybe I'm just all screwed up in the head. I don't know. But I never want to lie to you again. I don't ever want to take you for granted. Not ever. The heart attack was a wake-up call for me. I want to change. It can't be too late to forgive, can it? You may not want me back, but we still have these kids, you know?"

Rachel turned around to face me.

"I'll work out something for you to see the girls. Don't worry about that."

"You have to believe me. I love you, Rachel."

"Oh no. Please. Please, God. Don't say that" Rachel replied in disgust. Telling a person who's leaving you that you love her is just a really, really bad idea. If you had truly loved them, they would not be leaving. The right thing to say is that you were sorry that you had stopped loving them. Or that you didn't love them enough during in the past. Love as a verb is very different than love as a noun. We can feel love, but that is not the essence of what love really is. I know that now. But why did it have to take her leaving me and a heart attack to finally realize that I truly wanted to love her. To *love* her as a verb.

"I'll call you later this week and we can work out a schedule for the kids."

"Okay," I replied, knowing this could be the last time we would ever talk like this.

"And try to take care of yourself, okay?" she said sincerely.

"Hey, Rach?"

"What?"

"Can I tell you one more thing, really quick? Something I have learned."

Rachel fidgeted with the bag and I could tell that I had about ten seconds to try to find a way to keep her from leaving.

"I know that trust is important. You can trust me now. I'm really going to tell the truth from now on. No more exaggerating or little white lies. They are all the same and they are wrong. I just wanted you to know that, ... before you leave. I won't lie to you, ever again."

Rachel turned and looked at me again with a tiny spark of curiosity.

"Okay then, tell me. That day, that day that you somehow forgot about the birthday party, where were you?"

"Uh, well, you aren't ... I ... uh ..."

"That's what I thought," she said, turning abruptly to leave.

"No! Wait. I will tell you the truth. But it isn't that easy. See—"

"The truth, Neil? Where were you? You were an hour late and I doubt you just lost track of time walking the dog. You are never gone that long. Was it a rendezvous? A neighbor's wife? I need to know."

"Oh gosh, no. It wasn't anything like that. I barely know our neighbors. You know that."

"Then what? Tell me!" she implored.

"Okay. I will. But you aren't going to believe it," I said, trying to chuckle, so she would be prepared for the unbelievable explanation.

"Try me," she said.

I paced in a circle trying to come up with the words, and then I remembered that the best way to respond to a difficult question is to ask another one.

"What if I told you that I found a way to go back in time?"

"*Good God!*" Rachel exclaimed as she turned again to leave. I knew it sounded crazy, but I was not going to let her go without telling her about the house. She asked for the truth and she was going to get it. I walked three steps behind her as she walked out the door and toward her car.

"Please don't go just yet. Let me finish" I implored. "I don't know why or how, but there is this house—the one down the street with the green door, the abandoned one. You can go inside and . . . there are doors in the hallway and each one of them can take you back. Back in time. You can relive a moment in your life. You can't change anything, but you can see it again for what it really was or is, more clearly. You know, like watching a TV show over again. I've done it. That is where I was that day and I lost track of time, because . . . well, it's a time machine so—"

"They must have you on some really strong meds!" Rachel barked as she began to open the door to her car.

"I'm not on drugs! Wait, that's not true. I am on drugs, but most of this happened before . . . before the heart attack. I went back to some . . . events in my life. To relive them. And I swear to you, the house is a time machine and it is real. There is this guy named Dobie. He is kind of a spirit or ghost actually, but he helps you do it, like a guide."

I could tell from her expression that I was blowing it, so I put my leg in the way so Rachel could not close her car door.

"Please, Neil. I don't have time for this," Rachel said as she tried to shut her door.

"But I'm telling you the truth. I told you I'm not going to lie anymore. I was there today too, except I asked them to let me go forward. You don't want to do that. They warned me, but I did it anyway. Least not to a time when you aren't alive because your body will be dead, and you won't be able to sense anything. God, it was an awful feeling, but it made me want to be alive. As long as we are here and living, we can fix things. We can do that, Rachel. I know we can."

Rachel stopped and turned and looked at me closely. I knew she was trying to see if my eyes indicated some level of narcotic-induced hallucinogenic trance. It was clear to her that the words flowing from my mouth sounded like utter gibberish, but Rachel knew when I was lying and when I wasn't. Her perception skills were tremendous, and she had an uncanny ability to flush out the truth in me. So, even this crazy story was getting through a little, and that left her feeling truly puzzled.

"Okay. Let's say I believe this nonsense. Then where did you go? Where do you go in this time machine that was so important that you could just forget about your family?"

Aha! She was giving me an inch of leeway and I knew I had to be very careful with how I responded. I pondered which event from the house would be the best to describe.

"There were lots of trips back. Let me see . . . I think . . ."

"No. I want to know specifically where you went that day you missed the birthday party!" Rachel interrupted. "What was so important on that day that you had to disappoint our girls?"

Shit! She had to ask about that specific day as that was the one where I went back to be with that girl again, Cindy Wintergreen. I stammered to try to find a way out of this without lying to her again. In an effort to stay truthful, I avoided her direct question. "One time I went back to my graduation. When I won that award. That was pretty cool. Another time, just recently, Dobie made me into a baby and my dad was holding me and I actually peed in my diaper," I said through a nervous smile.

"Neil! I asked about the day you abandoned our girls. Where did you go that day?"

"I... I...." I was trapped and the momentary hesitation in my answer was all Rachel needed to make her move to close the door again. But my leg remained in the way.

"I, uh, I don't remember that day specifically too well. There was this girl from high school. That first one, you know? But it meant nothing. Afterward, I wished I hadn't done it. We were so young and—"

"You have got to be kidding me? I am so done here," Rachel said in a scratchy voice that meant she was about ready to scream.

"But I learned from it. There were other days that I—"

"That's enough of this. I'm leaving," she said as she closed the door again on my leg. In pain, I moved out of the way and she closed it completely. I knocked on the windshield of her car and shouted out to her.

"I'm trying to tell you the truth, Rachel!"

Rachel started the motor and slammed the car into reverse in a single deft motion. She was down the street as the words I had just uttered echoed back to me. *She must think I am completely nuts,* I thought. A house with a time machine?? Going back to be with an old girlfriend? Now she would really want to leave me. In addition to being a shitty husband, I was now an insane shitty husband who cheats. Not a good combination of traits.

Chapter 29

WHEN SOMEONE DIES, THE BOOK OF THEIR LIFE ON EARTH CLOSES FOREVER

Typically, unless you know people in Japan, when a phone rings at 4 a.m., there is good reason to worry. It is not likely to be good news. The best possible outcome is a wrong number, because no one calls anyone at this hour of night to just say hello. Even on those drunken nights when I would call an old girlfriend, it was always earlier than 4 a.m. So, when the phone rang and I saw that the time was 4:07 on my bedside clock, I knew immediately that something bad had happened. It took me three rings to get to the phone since it was on Rachel's side of the bed. I rubbed my eyes and took a deep breath before answering.

"Hello."

"Hey, bro. It's Chuck. You awake?"

"Not yet. What happened?"

"It's really bad news, Neil."

"I figured. Did Dad die?" I asked, thinking I already knew the answer.

"No," he said, his voice cracking. "It's Mom."

"Shit," I said, suddenly wishing that I had said something far more dignified upon hearing this tragic news.

"There was nothing they could do. She died right there in the house."

"Shit," I said again.

"Aunt Betty was going to call you, but I told her to let me do it. I'm gonna come over there now, okay?"

My Aunt Betty was my mother's only sibling, and she really looked up to my mother. Aunt Betty had gone through a lot recently as she had lost her husband just two years ago after a long battle with cancer. My mother comforted my aunt throughout the process, and they had grown even closer since my uncle's death. They seemed to be close in the same way that Chuck and me were. They were very different, but they needed each other. She had been calling my mother repeatedly the previous day and started to sense that something was wrong. After a dozen or so unanswered calls, Aunt Betty called the paramedics and they found my mother lying on the floor in her kitchen. They rushed her to the hospital, but she was pronounced dead at 3:25am. The cause of death was uncertain at the time, but I figured that my mother had just worn out.

"Sure. Come on over," I said softly, but the reality had still not sunk in. My mother was gone? Suddenly, I didn't know what to think. Was that why she was so tired and couldn't handle my father anymore? My mind was racing with thoughts of regret and fear of having lost the only parent that truly loved me. Like Rachel leaving, this would create another large gap in my life. One probably too big to ever be filled again.

"You there, bro?" Chuck asked. "Did you hear me? I'm coming over."

"Sure. Come on over. But wait ... do you know ... ? I mean, what are we supposed to do?"

"Aunt Betty asked us to come to Louisville right away. She'll meet us at Mom's house, and then we can go to the funeral home from there and make all the arrangements."

"So was she . . . ? What? How did she die?"

"I think she just stopped breathing, bro" Chuck stated somberly. "She was having some lung issues last week, but she has had those before. I guess it was just her time to go."

I could hardly believe it. My mother was dead. I rubbed my eyes a few times and then got up to start getting dressed. I had fallen asleep in my underwear and nothing else. Ever since Rachel left, the idea of wearing pajamas to bed just seemed stupid to me. And why did people wear special clothes to go to bed anyway? Seemed more logical to me to wear something like sweatpants and sneakers in case there was a fire and you had to run from the burning house.

As I dressed, I was completely unsure what I should be thinking. Everything felt surreal. I've seen scenes of people getting that type of phone call. I remembered one of the television shows Rachel and I used to watch had an episode where a lead male character died in a car wreck. During the dramatic episode, they showed the other character's reaction to the phone call when they heard the news. From silent shock to raging tears, the reactions were all different and I wondered how realistic any of the responses were. I had never been through something like that, but now it was happening to me. My mother was dead. And so far, all I could think of was this stupid television show.

When Chuck showed up, he looked like he had just stopped crying two minutes before I opened the door. Crying, even in private, leaves a mark on your face and people just know. We did a brief "guys hug," which I had invented to make us more comfortable with the idea of touching each other in a show of affection. Instead of a traditional hug, Chuck and I did a one-arm (fist closed) half-hug and half-chest bump. I thought it showed the proper amount of brotherly affection without looking girly. Chuck agreed that this was to be our signature hug for the remainder of our brotherly lives.

While waiting for Chuck to arrive, I had been looking all over the house for something to bring with me on our trip back to Louisville. It seemed logical to me that I should gather together some memorabilia or at least some pictures of my mother. What else do you do in times like this? I knew there would be moments of silent awkwardness as we were not a family that dealt very well with deep emotion. Do we speak of the good old days? Do we say nothing and just let the tears flow? I wasn't sure what I was feeling yet, except I was nervous and needed something to do to keep me busy. Yet, after a half hour of searching, the only thing I found that related to my mother was one picture in a drawer of her with my kids from five or six years ago. That was it. The woman who had raised me and the primary caregiver in my life was gone and all I seemed to have left to remember her was this one unframed picture. I couldn't help but instantly rethink my policy of not putting up pictures of family in my house.

Chuck followed me into my bedroom and his mouth was full of something.

"Hey, bro. You want some?"

Chuck waved a bag of doughnut holes in front of me, but I had no appetite. I shook my head.

"Let me get my bags and we'll leave in ten," I said. Chuck took a sip of his coffee and wandered out into the hallway looking at a series of scenic paintings on the wall.

"I can't believe she's gone," Chuck offered up to break the silence. "Fuck. She was only seventy-eight. Heck, man. That's not too many years away for us, bro. Hey, Neil, why do you guys have a painting of a bunch of dead flowers?"

"They are dried flowers, idiot," I shouted out to Chuck. I started to pack my travel bag the way I always did. I would literally dress myself as I packed so I wouldn't forget any of the essentials. Underwear first. Socks. Pants. Shirt. Belt. I would multiply by the number of days that I would be gone so I wouldn't have to wear anything more than once, and this was generally a very good way to pack. Except this time, I had no idea what to wear. What would we be doing? How many days would I be gone? What type of clothes would I need? For a moment, I couldn't even remember what month it was and whether to dress for cold or hot weather. My brain was in an immense fog.

"You think the guy would want to paint something with living flowers? That's all I'm saying. Did that frizzy-haired guy on TV do these?"

Bob Ross was the artist on PBS that painted those scenic portraits using only a putty knife. He would literally whip the edge of the knife across the canvas and instantly a beautiful snow-capped mountain would appear. He seemed like a really nice guy, and he loved saying things like "Let's put some silly little trees here and here. These are happy trees and you can decide where they live. It's your world. You get to choose." I would be mesmerized when I watched him paint a beautifully detailed mountain scene in less than three minutes.

"Don't forget to bring your dark suit!" Chuck yelled out.

"Oh yeah. Thanks," I called back. I would have forgotten it had he not said something.

I had not dressed in a suit or a tie in years. I wasn't even sure where I kept my suits as there was never a cause to wear one for business anymore. I went into the guest room closet and found a dark-gray suit that I thought looked more appropriate than my blue one for a funeral. I knew it would need pressing when I got there, so I just folded it up and shoved it into my duffel bag. I looked at the ties that were hanging on a closet hook and picked a somber-looking blue one and shoved that in on top of the suit. As I went to zip up the bag, I thought of the feeling I had when I had asked Dobie to let me go to my own funeral. Was my mother in that state now? That state of nothingness?

Or would she be able to come back and watch her own funeral as I had wanted to do?

I grabbed the bag and went back to my bedroom to get all the other essentials I would need. Wallet. An extra pair of socks just in case. A book to read from beside the bed. I took some spare change from the jar on the nightstand in case we needed it for tolls. As hard as I tried, I couldn't remember if there were any tolls roads on the way from Cleveland to Louisville. What else would I need? As I crossed in front of the mirror above the dresser, I saw my reflection and it didn't look anything like I expected. I stopped and looked more intensely at myself and saw… an old man. I had lost even more of my hair during my illness. I had wrinkles under my eyes that I had never noticed before. The weight loss had made me look even older as the skin under my neck now sagged. There was an age spot … or a liver spot—whatever you want to call it on my right cheek. I looked old. But the strangest part of all was that for the first time in my life I looked a lot like my father.

I couldn't help then but think about my dad. Who would take care of him now? Would he even understand that Mom was gone? Should we even tell him? What would he do without my mother around to visit and take care of him?

"Come on, Alice. Let's roll!" Chuck pleaded as he walked down the stairs.

As I started to move away from the mirror, I felt a drop of moisture in my nostril. Then another, and then another. I was starting to cry, but I had no control over the tears. I wasn't thinking sad thoughts. I wasn't really thinking of anything except how I looked, and then the dam broke. Before I knew it, I was bawling. The tears streamed down my face and I hit my knees. I was crying so hard; it was difficult to breathe. Chuck came to the edge of the stairs, but he knew not to come up. I was temporarily inconsolable. My guess is that he had just gone through the same thing during his car ride to my place. It was the inevitable and visceral reaction to the truth that life—every life—does come to an end. My mother was gone and whatever she and I had done and or said during our lives was now history. It could not be changed, and the book on her life was closed forever.

I grabbed my cell phone and thought that this might be a good reason to call Rachel. Maybe she would feel sorry for me and that would help us to reconnect a little. She knew how much my mother meant to me. I sat down on the bed to call when Chuck yelled again from the living room.

"Come on, dude. Pack your tampons and let's go! We need to be down there by one to meet Aunt Betty."

"I'm coming. Just give me one more minute," I responded.

I scrolled down my contacts list to Rachel's cell phone number but realized that it was still too early in the morning to call her. And then I thought that a text would be more appropriate and that she could call me when she heard the news. I began the text: *Rachel. So sorry to tell you this by text, but my mother passed away last night. I'm heading to Louisville now with Chuck and I don't know how long I will be gone. You can reach me on my cell phone if you need me. Sorry to pass on such sad news. Neil.*

There. That was perfect. She would have to call when she got this. I didn't pressure her to go there as I had no idea what would be happening and when. Anyway, she would do what was right. Rachel always did the right thing in these types of circumstances. The problem for me is that I had no idea what the right thing was. I had never lost anyone so close to me before. My grandparents had all passed away and that was sad but losing my mother would be different. I knew that. She was such a big part of my life and now she was gone. And even though we had not been talking much the past few years, I knew losing her was going to be difficult. Without my mother, my wife, kids, and, yes, even the dog, I would be more alone than I ever thought possible.

Chapter 30

THERE ARE TIMES IN LIFE WHEN YOU JUST CAN'T CRY ANYMORE

They lowered the casket into the ground so slowly that I wanted to yell "Hurry the hell up before someone else dies." There was no need to dramatize the process of burying a dead person. The casket did not contain my mother. When I saw her body at the funeral home, I knew she was not inside of it. It looked so different than a live person. All that was really left was a corpse that drew some resemblance to my mother. The expression and personality were not there in her face. The life or spirit that made that body my mother was absent.

"Let's go, dear," my Aunt Betty said, taking my arm. We walked slowly away from the cemetery and said nothing. I had cried all the tears that my body would allow me to cry. There were no more left. I had seen people at funerals before who had lost children and spouses, but I didn't understand, until now, why they didn't show more emotion. Whatever emotion they had was gone for that moment, and the body was in a state of self-preservation. I couldn't have cried again if I wanted to. My brother Chuck delivered the eulogy and I could tell that he was completely cried out too. Unlike me, Chuck was an entertaining public speaker, but this was different, and he knew not to try to be too funny. But what he did say was perfect and very touching—especially for Chuck.

"As most of you know, my mother's life could be summed up in just one word: generosity. She only thought of others and that is a fact.

She was a great friend to everyone she met, and she always seemed to have the energy and time to help someone in need. She was also a saint for putting up with my dad and my deranged younger brother."

The people in the church laughed somberly and Chuck smiled. I didn't mind the *deranged* reference. He was right.

"My mother was quite simply the anchor for our family. Without her, my father would have been lost. It was her strength that allowed him to appear so strong. She was the one that made the phone calls to sick parishioners. She hosted the staff get-togethers as my father would have been terrible at those things. She made everyone she knew feel loved and appreciated. She did all that without ever asking what was in it for her. It was no secret to my dad. My mother made up for my father's deficiencies and he cherished her for that."

Suddenly I knew for the first time in my life that Chuck had some of the same issues with my father that I did. But he was so much less obvious about it than me.

"Some of you are aware that my father is now in a special memory-loss facility. That's why he is not here with us today. My mother must have known that he needed to be specially cared for after she was gone. Only my mother really knew the real person inside of him. But I know this. She loved my father and she loved him with all her heart. I'm not sure how God evaluates us at the end of our lives, but it could be in terms of how much love we gave out. And my mother was about loving people and helping them find a way to be happier."

Chuck paused for what seemed like a full minute and then continued.

"My father started to lose his mental faculties five or six years ago, and my mother did everything she could for him. I'm not sure I ever thanked her enough for doing all of that on her own. Frankly, I wasn't ever aware of it and I feel terrible about that now. I wish she could be here now, so I could thank her. I should have thanked her more for being such a good mother as well as a good friend and sister to Aunt Betty. But I can do it now. We all can because she is with us in spirit and listening to me right now ... or I think she is."

Aha! Even Chuck agreed that we get to listen in on our own funeral!

Chuck looked up to the sky and continued, "So, uh, thanks, Mom. Thanks, from me and from all the other people here and elsewhere that you touched during your life. I'm going to miss you."

Chuck started to slowly start back to his seat before pausing and starting to smile.

"Oh, ... and those funny looking cigarettes you found in the house when I was a teenager ... those weren't mine, I swear."

Most everyone assembled laughed as Chuck walked slowly back to his seat. I knew he would have to get in one humorous anecdote and I'm glad he did. It's always good to ease the tension at somber events like this and that comment worked. As we sat there in silence, his words were still echoing in my brain. Mom was in heaven. And that is where we are all heading in this life, we hope. God just needs to get us ready and maybe—just maybe—that is what all of this crap is about. The trials, the pain, the separation, it's all to get us ready to be with God in heaven. Maybe that is why the green-door house was showing me so many painful experiences. Like a good can of spray paint, I needed to be shaken up before I could paint something meaningful. As I helped my aunt into the car, I felt a gentle touch on my arm from behind me. I turned around and saw Rachel standing there in a beautiful black dress with white lace trim.

"Are you okay?" she asked as I resisted the urge to pull her into my arms. I hadn't seen her in the church, but I knew she was coming to the funeral. She had called and left a message that once again revealed her ability to always do and say the right thing.

"I'm fine, but . . . it is so good to see you here. Where are the girls?" I responded as I took her hand in mine.

"They're waiting in the car. They're okay. I told them that I needed to talk with you."

"Well, now is not the best time. Can you come to the parish hall? They're going to have some cake and food, or something. Maybe some booze too, I'm not sure."

"Sure," she said, and she brushed me gently on my left arm. "I loved what Chuck said. Your mother was a saint. He got that part right, for sure."

At that moment, I wanted to reach out and pull Rachel so close that she could never escape my grasp. She knew about the difficulty I had with my father and that my mother compensated for him the best she could. She also knew this was a huge loss for me and that I was going to need help. I needed Rachel badly, and I wanted her back in my life. But with a warm smile and a pat on my arm, she turned and walked away.

I got into the black limousine and saw that my Aunt Betty was holding Chuck's hand and was staring blankly out the window. She was my mother's younger sister by nine years, and this loss would only add to her current list of sorrows. With the age difference, my mother was almost like a parent to her too. And like me, it looked as if she wanted to cry but couldn't. Chuck looked at me with panic in his eyes as if to say *Do or say something!* So I slid over into the seat opposite my aunt and reached over and took her other hand.

"I'm so sorry, Aunt Betty. I'm really sorry."

My aunt squeezed my hand and smiled.

"I know. I'm sorry too," she said wistfully. "I just wish I had been there when she passed. She was all alone."

Aunt Betty continued to gaze out the window as I fidgeted. I wanted to choose the right words to comfort her, but I had no experience with this. So I just tried to imagine what my mother would have said.

"You know, Aunt B . . . (Yes, we called her that because of the character on *The Andy Griffith Show*. I had forgotten how much she hated that reference, so I was not off to a good start.) You and my mom are like me and Chuck. We pretty much go through everything together."

I looked over at Chuck who shrugged his shoulders to indicate his disdain for my sentimentality. I ignored him the best I could and continued.

"I know you're going to miss her. But the way I figure it, we can all be in this together. Me and Chuck and you. We can help each other, you know? And if you ever need anything, we will be there. I promise."

Chuck looked at me again as if to say *Why'd you have to bring me into this?* But he knew that the exact words were not that important. It was more important that we commit to stay in touch with Aunt Betty. She would need us, and we needed to make sure she was still a part of our lives. My mother would have wanted that.

And I knew something else my mother would have wanted. And she would have said it to me and to me only. And those words would have been, *Please take good care of your father.*

Chapter 31

THE MOST IMPORTANT OF ALL VIRTUES ARE FAITH, HOPE, AND LOVE,

When I got back to Cleveland, I went to the house with the green door, but for the first time since this all started, the door was locked. I looked inside, and all the furniture was gone. I knocked on the door and waited but heard nothing. During the drive back from Louisville, I had told myself that I needed to go back to the house one more time. I wanted to return to the day that Rachel and I got married. I wanted to see if there was anything from that day that I could learn that would help me understand what went wrong. When did we steer off course? I knocked again and again and still...nothing. At that moment, I wondered if all that had gone on in this house had just been an illusion or in my imagination.

I started to turn to walk back home, and then the front door made a sound. It was a creaking sound that was like the noise a new house makes when it is settling into the foundation. And then the door opened a crack and I walked into the foyer. I looked down the hallway and saw that all the doors were closed except for one. The door that had the broken doorknob on it was slightly ajar. I called out for Dobie.

"Hey, Dobie, where are you? I need you, buddy."

When Dobie didn't respond, I looked back at the open door. Could he be down there? I looked down the staircase.

"Dobie? You there?"

I walked down the first few stairs, but hesitated and thought, *What the heck is happening here?* It was freezing cold in the stairway and the sounds were again very creepy. I decided to go down just another few steps and within seconds, I was back in the church where Rachel and I were married. I was standing at the same altar where we stood so many years ago with Chuck, my best man, a few feet to my left in his black tuxedo. My father was in front of us as he would be the minister for the service. Rachel was poised at the back of the church next to her father. She was dressed in a flowing ivory-colored gown, but I had not remembered that Rachel wore a piece of blue ribbon in her hair that day. The blue ribbon was a piece of material from a prize I had won for her on our first date.

And then I immediately remembered. Rachel and I had been set up by Chuck's wife at the time. He convinced Debbie to get us together as he thought Rachel would be someone I would like. He was right. She was totally my type. I thought a small carnival would be a good place to get to know her, and there would be plenty of things to do to keep us from awkward conversations. After riding the Ferris wheel and eating a couple of corn dogs (no longer on my new diet), we walked down the long row of midway games. This was the type of temporary carnival that offered temptations for the guy to show off by trying to shoot a basketball into a hoop that was actually smaller than the ball itself or to knock over a stack of pins that weighed a thousand pounds each with a whiffle ball. No, I was not going to be suckered into their trap, but when Rachel saw a four-foot-tall stuffed giraffe in one of the booths and emanated *"aaahhhwww,"* I knew then and there that I had to win her that giraffe.

The game "ring toss" was one where you had to toss a light wooden bamboo ring around various-size pegs in the center of the booth. It was a little like the concept of horseshoes. If the ring successfully wrapped around the peg and dropped to the bottom, you would win a prize. The larger the width of the peg, the bigger the prize. To win the four-foot giraffe, I would need to ring the largest of the pegs. The carnival employee showed us that the ring would fit, but to get it to drop to the bottom would require a throw of tremendous skill and agility. I surmised that the ring toss would have to come from directly above the peg and not from the horizontal direction that I would be throwing it. As you would suspect, it was nearly impossible. Nevertheless, I gave the guy my two dollars and prepared to throw the first of the three rings.

Thirty dollars later, I asked the carnival guy again to prove to me that the ring would indeed fit around the largest peg. Rachel laughed as he once again demonstrated the ring fitting over the large peg. I felt like it was time to quit, but I gave him two more dollars, which would mean that I would have spent thirty-two dollars for a stuffed giraffe that I could have gotten at Walmart for ten bucks. But I had a new strategy this time, which was to toss the ring straight up toward the roof of the tent above the prizes. The likelihood of success here was literally one in a thousand, but at least there was a chance. I took the first of three rings and tried to determine the exact spot on the roof of the tent to aim at to get the ring to fall in the appropriate fashion to go around the peg. I took the first ring and threw it and hit the spot perfectly. The ring fell as I hoped it would, directly down onto the peg. I started to jump for joy, but the ring only dropped part of the way down the peg. There it sat at a forty-five-degree angle, halfway down. I looked helplessly at the carnival guy who shook his head.

"Come on!" I pleaded.

"Gotta go all the way to the bottom," he grunted while pulling the ring off the wooden peg to remove any evidence of how close I had come. "Ya got two more tries."

I took the next ring and tried again but didn't come close. Rachel looked over at me with playful admiration as I proudly held up the last ring.

"This is it!" I said. "If I make it, we take all the winnings, get married, and move to Costa Rica."

"Sure," Rachel replied with a smile. "That is, I'm sure you can't do it."

I took the ring and tossed it underhand toward the ceiling. This time it actually bounced off the top of the tent and sailed down toward the peg. When it first hit the peg, it was at a slight angle and it looked like it wouldn't make it, but then a slight breeze seemed to flow in at just the right time and the ring straightened out and down it slid. Down, down, down, and . . . down to the bottom.

"We got a winner!" the carnival man shouted out as he rang an annoying bell.

Rachel jumped up and down with delight. I smiled and bowed to the people around us as the carnival man grabbed the ring.

"You can pick a prize now," he said.

"She wants the giraffe," I stated, pointing to the tall yellowish figure behind him.

"Can't do that one," the midway man said with a smirk. "You gotta ring all three to get the giraffe," he said, putting the ring back down on the table in front of us. Rachel burst into laughter.

"Unbelievable. I'd have a better chance winning the lottery three times in a row," I joked.

"You can pick any of the prizes here," the carnival man said, pointing to a row of smaller stuffed animals.

As I surveyed the choices, I looked at Rachel and said, "You pick one."

"I'll take the bear," she said, pointing at a little brown bear that had a blue ribbon wrapped around its neck that read, *I love you*.

The carnival man grabbed the bear off the shelf and gave it straight to Rachel. She put it in her arms and coddled it like a baby.

"Look at that. Here's our first child," she said while pulling the bear close to her chest.

"He's awfully hairy for a newborn," I remarked as I took her by the arm to leave.

"It's a she and she's perfect," Rachel responded happily as we walked back down the midway.

I knew right then and there that I would end up marrying this woman. We were only two hours into our first date, but it seemed like we had been friends for years. I was comfortable with her and I didn't feel the need to build myself up. She seemed to know me already, warts and all, and the warts didn't matter to her. At the end of that night, when I dropped her off at her apartment, she smiled at me before getting out of the car. This was normally the time in a date when I was most nervous. What do I do? Walk her up to the door? Do I kiss her? If so, on the cheek or a quick peck on the mouth? What if she asked me in? Did I even want to come in?

"I had a good time," she said as she got out of her side of the car.

Without thinking, I scrambled to get out of my side and around the car as quickly as I could. I decided I would walk her to the door and that was it. I did not want to go in. It had been a perfect date and I didn't want to ruin it. I just needed to think of the right thing to say, but my mind was blank. We walked quietly toward the door and then it came to me. It was instinctive, and I had never said it before, but I went with my gut. As Rachel dug in her purse for her keys, I stood just a foot away and faced her.

"Rachel, would it be okay if I kissed you good night?"

She looked up at me and smiled. She was just as surprised as me that I was asking for permission to kiss her. I mean, who does that?

"Sure. That would be nice. You may kiss me, sire," she responded, and we kissed one good closed-mouth kiss on the lips.

That was it, but it was perfect. I smiled before turning around and walking back to the car. I looked down once at the sidewalk to make sure I wouldn't trip on anything as she watched me. When I got to the car, I turned to see for sure that she got inside the apartment safely. She waved a sweet little goodbye to me as she slipped inside. It was one of the warmest and happiest moments of my life. I had found my future wife.

And there she was again. Sixty or so feet away at the back of the church. And in her hair was that little blue ribbon from the bear. As she and her father approached the altar, I felt a wave of emotion rise from my gut and into my throat. I loved this woman. How could I have ever let her leave me, or even give her a reason to think of leaving? She got closer and closer and then we were side by side. But something felt weird. I wasn't sweating like I did the first time. I actually felt fairly comfortable. And unlike all the other times I had gone back in time, when I smiled at her, it seemed to be the present me smiling. When I lifted my hand out to clasp hers, it seemed to be my decision. I even thought of winking at her to see if I was truly controlling my actions, but I didn't want to look stupid, so I just smiled. And Rachel smiled back as she lifted her veil and tugged playfully on the little blue ribbon.

"Dearly beloved," my father began. To my amazement, he seemed genuinely happy to be marrying us. And it was great to see him with all his faculties again.

"We are gathered here in this house of God to join these two young people in the bonds of holy matrimony."

As my father continued, I squeezed Rachel's hand and she looked over at me curiously. I couldn't resist the temptation to whisper a little something to her. Even though I knew I couldn't, I looked through my younger self and tried to whisper the words *I'm sorry*. But strangely, I thought I heard the words. It was faint, but I was sure I heard something. Had I had broken through somehow? Rachel then squeezed my hand back and I thought I saw her mouth the words, *I know*".

"Do you, Neil, take this woman to be your wife? To have and to hold. For richer and poorer. In sickness and in health. To love and to cherish all the days of your life?"

"I really do," I responded, which drew a few laughs from the congregation. But had I said that the first time? I didn't remember the *really* part at all. Then my father turned to Rachel.

"Do you, Rachel, take this man to be your husband? To have and to hold? For richer and poorer? In sickness and in health? To love and to cherish all the days of your life?"

Rachel looked down at our clasped hands and hesitated. Now I knew that something was wrong. This was different. Her eyes were anxiously darting back and forth. This was not what I remembered. She looked so scared. Things were changing. Was she going to say no? Could God be giving her the chance to change her mind? To change everything? Would this erase the last seventeen years of our life together. Then the worst thought of all crossed my mind: What would happen to our children? How could we adopt those two amazing girls if we were not together? I looked at Rachel with a desperate fear that seemed close to engulfing me. My body began to feel weak and I started to feel that feeling . . . that feeling like I was going to pass out as I had in the sixth grade. Without thinking, I looked out into the congregation and saw my mother nodding reassuringly at me. My mother was there and somehow seemed to know exactly what I was feeling. I knew then what I had to do.

"Are you okay?" Rachel said to me as I slowly regained my bearings. Rachel looked into my eyes closely and squeezed my hands even harder. In that moment, I knew this was where everything had been leading me these past few months. This was it! That's what this house had been about. I straightened myself up to stand face to face and eye to eye with the person I hoped would soon be my wife.

"Rachel," I said confidently. "I promise you, I will be a good husband. I only want to make you happy. Please believe me. I love you and will love you the rest of my life. This time I really mean it."

The words had seemed to simply leak from my mind and out of my mouth. I wasn't saying the words so much as I was feeling them. The congregation stared in awe as the sincerity of my words lingered in the air. Rachel smiled and looked down briefly and then back up at me.

"I believe you, I think," she said, and then a small smile came across her face. It was a smile I hadn't seen in so very long.

"Then do you?" my father directed to Rachel.

"Okay. Yes. I will marry him. I do."

Chuck then took the rings out of his pocket and handed them to me. We put them on and I grabbed Rachel's hands and looked deeply into her eyes. She could not have looked more beautiful to me than she did at that moment.

"Well then," my father continued, "by the power vested in me on this day in the city of Cleveland, I now pronounce you . . . husband and wife."

I embraced and kissed Rachel the same way I had done that night at her apartment. We turned and walked down the aisle toward the back of the church. I couldn't resist looking at her the entire way, but I was still not sure if this was really happening. When we walked through the back doors, I touched her face and her smile reappeared.

"Is that you in there? Are you for real?" I asked as I pulled her closer.

"Did you mean it? Did you really mean it?" Rachel asked, pushing me back slightly.

"Mean what?"

"That you will make it better this time?"

"Yes. Of course, I will. Wait, what do you mean, this time?" I asked.

"I just need to know that you will try harder. I will try harder, too," Rachel replied.

"I promise. I will ... but ..."

Rachel turned away from me, but I moved around to face her and looked deeply into her dark brown eyes.

"Okay, okay," she said, pushing me back. "I just hope you mean it. We can't let things get like they were with us ever again. I can't live like that."

"Me neither. But how ...? Wait ..."

I looked around as the people began to file out of the church. As they approached us, I pulled Rachel into a small alcove where I knew we could get another few seconds of privacy.

"Are you ... I mean, did this ...? What just happened here?"

"I got curious," Rachel said. "I heard what you said about the house, so I went to check it out."

I stared at her in disbelief. She had gone into the time machine. We were both back in time and she had chosen the same broken door that I had.

"So, this is us. We are ..." I tried to finish, but I didn't have the words.

"I want to trust you, Neil, but we both have some work to do. I need to change too. I know I am tough on you. My father was always so distant from my mother, and I wanted to make sure that didn't happen with us. So I pushed you. I'll try to ease up a bit."

"No. I want you to stay just the way you are. Don't change anything. I want to be pushed. I think I need to be pushed actually," I stated with conviction.

I pulled her close again and we began to kiss. We both closed our eyes tightly and when we opened them, we were back in the green-door house. We were in the empty room in front and were back to the current day. I kissed her again and then realized that Dobie was standing directly across from us.

"Well, kids, what did you think?" Dobie asked cheerfully.

"Pretty wild," Rachel said as she took my hand.

Dobie smiled as the sun shone toward him and brightened his face.

"But you warned me about that broken door. Did we do anything to mess up our future?" I asked.

"No. We controlled it and the future outcomes were not impacted. Cloyde was adamant that we kept all the new interactions between the two of you and no one else."

"So the girls?" Rachel asked.

"They are back at the house with Chuck. Waiting for you."

We both sighed with relief.

"Cloyde, huh? Will we ever get to meet this guy, Cloyde?" I asked half-jokingly.

"You will someday. I'm sure of that," Dobie said with a smile.

"Well then, I think we are done here," I remarked as I opened the front door and let Rachel cross in front of me. I looked back and saw Dobie standing proudly with his hands in his pockets of his brown striped slacks. It was then that I realized that I had that feeling again—that feeling of making the impossible catch or long run. The unbelievable feeling you get when you first hold your child in your arms, and you know you have done something incredible. All this was impossible, but it had happened and the joy I felt was just amazing. But I also knew there would be tough times again. It would take work to keep it this way and I was willing to do all it took to make that happen.

"Thanks, Dobie. Thanks for everything," I said quietly.

"Yes, thank you. That was quite an experience," Rachel added.

"You two be good to each other. Oh Neil, wait. I have something for you."

I stopped, and Dobie walked toward me and handed me the brass doorknob from the broken door.

"I thought you might like to keep this. As a souvenir," he stated with a smile.

"Thanks, Dobie. I will put it on the mantle, so we never forget what happened here."

"Good," he stated firmly. "Take care now."

"You too," I said as I slowly closed the green door.

When we reached the end of the front walkway, Rachel and I simultaneously turned to look back at the old house. Then she took my hand in hers and smiled before saying, "Let's go see the kids."

Epilogue

It was a few months later when they started to tear down the old abandoned house. The entire family and even the dog watched as they knocked down the walls and dragged the dusty remains into dumpsters. Rachel looked over at me and winked as the dog sniffed the grass near the front walk. I had related to her about all the experiences I had gone through at the house and that I was still learning from each of them. Turns out Rachel had gone back to a few other places in her life too. We would laugh together about whether it had really happened or if we were just crazy. But things were pretty good with us now, and we were both committed to keeping it that way.

No, things weren't perfect, but are they ever? I missed my mother terribly, but I could tell that there was a part of her that was still living on in me; the same way a part of me will live on in my kids. And now I had my father to take care of too. Chuck and I agreed that it would be best to move him into a qualified care facility near us and we found a good one just a few miles away. Now that he was close by, our goal was for one of us to visit him at least every other day. He was aware that my mother was now gone, but he seemed to be adjusting to his new environment very nicely. We finally seemed to be comfortable around each other. He still doesn't say much, but I know he appreciates me being there even if we just watch television.

It took me a long time to figure this out, but life is a lot simpler than I once thought. It isn't about me. It is about doing what I can to help others. This was the thing that made me successful at my job, and it would work well in the rest of my relationships. It was that green-door house that got my wife and me back together (with the help of Dobie and Cloyde), and I knew that our lives were going to change for the better. Like my mother, when I die, I want to be remembered as having been there when people needed me. My father needed me now, and I intend to be there for him no matter what. Chuck and I also pledged to Aunt Betty that she would always be expected in our homes for the holidays. She even offered to take care of Chuck's kids from time to time which will be good for Chuck and I suspect the kids as well.

Eventually, I opened that package that came to the house from Rachel. It was a picture of the four of us from our last vacation in Florida. Rachel had it blown up and framed and we now display it proudly on our mantle next to the old brass doorknob and a picture of my parents.

I reached over and held Mary's hand, and then pulled Jessica closer to me as the bulldozers knocked down another wall of the old home. Jessica tugged on my shirt as a dust cloud rose upward from the scattered debris.

"Daddy?"

"Yes, honey?" I replied.

"Why'd they have to tear the old house down? Couldn't they have just fixed it back up?"

"Oh, I don't know," I replied. "I guess the old house did its job, but sometimes it is good to start over and build something new."

"Like you and Mommy?" Mary asked.

The pure innocence and innate intelligence of children is remarkable, isn't it?

"Yep. Like me and Mommy."

Rachel smiled at me as Dingo tugged on her leash for us to get moving. I took one last look at what was left of the old house and thought of Dobie. I wondered if he might be watching, so I gave the house a quick wave just in case. And then we all headed for home.

CPSIA information can be obtained
at www.ICGtesting.com
Printed in the USA
FSHW011146060820
72725FS